Thatcher

ROBINSON DESTRUCTION BOOK 1

KATHI S. BARTON

This is a work of fiction. Names, characters, places, and incidents are products of the author's imagination or are used fictitiously and are not to be construed as real. Any resemblance to actual events, locations, organizations, or persons, living or dead, is entirely coincidental.

World Castle Publishing, LLC
Pensacola, Florida
Copyright © Kathi S. Barton 2019
Paperback ISBN: 9781949812602
eBook ISBN: 9781949812619
First Edition World Castle Publishing, LLC, January 21, 2019
http://www.worldcastlepublishing.com
Licensing Notes
All rights reserved. No part of this book may be used or reproduced in any manner whatsoever without written permission, except in the case of brief quotations embodied in articles and reviews.
Cover: Karen Fuller
Editor: Maxine Bringenberg

Chapter 1

An early morning run was her favorite thing. Rogen felt like she was free when she was out in the time between darkness and when the sun crested over the hills in her new town. Whatever happened here, it was going to be because that was what she wanted, and not what she had no control over. She and her brother Jamie were here for a fresh start, where no one cared where they came from. At least that was their hope.

A familiar car drove by her and she waved. Every morning about this time she'd see the family go by her on her weekday runs. She liked to imagine that they were taking the children to school and to daycare as the parents made their way to their jobs. There were two car seats in the back seat with babies in them. They were tiny, snuggled up in the seats every morning. The child, she didn't know the sex, was the most enthusiastic waver she'd ever seen.

As they passed her by, she continued her run. Ten miles out, ten back. Then she'd shower, eat, and get on with her job. The running not only kept her in shape but got her out of the house at least once a day. Rogen not only worked from home, but she seldom left it either. She thought that was why this meant so much to her.

The sound of metal against metal ripped through the silence of the morning. Before she could get her bearings on where it might have come from, a different car sped by her. Rogen took note of the license plate number and the state. The driver was laughing hard as he or she nearly took Rogen out by swerving to try and hit her. She didn't know the person, but she would find out who it was when she got home.

Continuing on her run after texting the number to herself, she put her phone back in her pocket. She knew that if she didn't do it right away, make a note of the plate number, she'd never remember it when she got home.

Just as she rounded the bend toward the long stretch of nothing but fields, she saw the overturned car with the family inside. Hurrying to the car, she could see that the man was hurt badly. Rogen made a mental note that he'd been shot in the left shoulder. Not wasting any time, she pulled her knife out of her sock pocket and cut him free of the belt that had him strapped upside down in the car. The smell of gasoline was making itself known to her, and she knew that she had to hurry.

Dragging his body to the other side of the road from where the accident was, she rushed back for the woman. Rogen thought that if she could get the adults out, it would be easier for her to save the kids, as the big front window was gone.

The woman was alive but that's about all she knew. Cutting her free of the seat belts, Rogen also grabbed her purse. She then scolded herself all the way, while taking her to her husband, that it wasn't like she was going shopping or anything. But it seemed right, somehow, that she had her purse, so she let it go.

The children in the seats were screaming. And just as she was starting to cut the first one loose from the seat, she saw the other car coming back. This time the person paused long enough to throw something at the car. The explosion knocked her forward when whatever was tossed at the car ignited the gas. The power of the blast from it had her landing on the middle child.

Rogen must have blacked out for a moment or two. When she woke, she knew that she'd been burnt, and badly, judging by how it hurt her to the point of nearly being sick every time she moved. But she had to save the kids before the gas tank blew too.

The car seats were somehow strapped to the car. She tried and tried to get one of them loose, but it was too much for her with her back and arms hurting so badly. Taking her knife out again, cutting the things over the child's shoulders and lap, she took the baby from the seat and set it right outside the car, and reached for the other one.

It went faster this time, getting the baby out and at least in her arms. Rogen was on fire now, literally. Her clothing was sticking to her back so badly that she knew that she'd be in trouble with this. Taking the babies to where their parents were, she laid them down and put the sucker things — binkies, she thought they were called — into their mouths. Thankfully they'd been pinned to their blankets. The silence was golden for a few minutes, then Rogen went back for the other child.

The gasoline was a huge puddle under the car and trailing down the street. If the flames from the rubber on the tire got to it, everything, including her and the boy, would go up with it. Rogen hurried as best she could.

Limping badly now, she made her way back to the little boy. He was still unconscious, and Rogen could see that he had a few burn marks on his hands. Cutting him loose, she tried to pick him up but she hurt too badly. Crying now, she tried to drag him from the car using her one hand. The other, she noticed, was red and full of dark blisters.

The ticking of something was all the notice that she got before the back end of the car exploded. She knew that she'd been lifted up and tossed away with the young boy in her arms, and all she could think about was that she'd failed him. He'd not wave at her any more.

Waking up the second time, she realized that she'd been tossed from the car. Lucky for her and the little boy, he'd been in her arms. Moving cautiously, she tried to stand but her legs were no longer working, it seemed.

He was burnt now. The back of his arms and legs were red like hers, but he didn't seem to be blistered. Rogen sobbed for the family. She felt like she'd failed them all by getting the little boy hurt. In the back of her mind she knew that was stupid, that she'd gotten them all out, but she didn't like to fail. Failure meant that someone always got the shaft, usually her.

Standing up as best she could, she dragged him by his leg to his family. The babies were still crying but not nearly as badly as before. Had they been in the car when it blew the second time, they would have died. The blast would have hit them full in the face, as they had been turned facing the explosion. Thankful that she'd been able to save them from dying, Rogen started to feel every single burn on her body.

The car was on fire, just a shell of what it had been. Rogen had lost her cell phone and couldn't call for help. With the remote area that it had happened in, no one would see it for hours, she thought. Dropping to her knees on the road, she could see that there was nothing left for her to try and get out for them.

Just as she was ready to go back to them, a car came down the road and she thought perhaps she'd not hurt as badly if they just ran over her. Rogen stayed where she was, propped up only by exhaustion.

"My goodness, what happened here?" The man looked slightly familiar, but she couldn't think beyond the pain. "Honey, I'm going to lay you down on the grass over—"

"Thatch, they're here. The Conrads are here together. Oh, Thatch, I think she saved them all." The man looked at her and asked her what her name was. She didn't know. "She's Rogen something. I don't know her last name. She's not well, Thatch."

"No, I can see that." She was picked up, the scream from her mouth so painful to her that she just let it go. The man was still talking, but Rogen was beyond understanding him. She just hoped that someone would please forgive her for not getting them out sooner.

Rogen woke twice more, once to hear the man saying her name and asking her if she had any relatives to call. Just her brother, she wanted to say, but faded out again. The next time she woke it was to find a large tiger standing over her. Rogen was sure that she was dead—the pain in her body was gone.

Closing her eyes, Rogen knew that she was dead for sure. The big tiger was going to eat her up. She just hoped that he didn't mind his meal being well done.

~*~

"What in blue blazes are you doing, Maggie? She's hurt enough." She told him that she was going to save her. "Save her? Holy pin cushions, woman, she's nearly dead now.

You'll only make it worse for her. Leave her to die in peace. She did a good thing here and should be able to die without more pain."

His mate was the prettiest tiger he'd ever seen, and he was amazed by her every time he saw her. But this wasn't going to work, he just knew it. Thatch could hear the poor woman's heart getting slower with every breath she took. The poor girl would never stand a chance if bitten by a tiger too.

The first bite that Maggie gave the young woman didn't even make her scream. He knew that it had to be painful to her, but the poor thing was so far gone now that it didn't faze her. As he kept watch over the two babies, his wife moved down to Rogen's leg and bit her there.

Maggie would have to work fast now, or she'd lose her. But when the woman started to breathe a little better, her heart just a bit stronger, Maggie looked at him. He knew what she was going to ask him, even before she reached out through their link.

Help me. You used to be a leader, Thatch. Your help would make her stronger. Help me save her. Putting down the little girl he'd been holding, Thatch took off his shirt. *You're a good man, have I told you that lately?*

"Don't be trying to butter me up now. You know as well as I do that someday she's going to meet her mate, and he won't have a thing to do with her because she's a tiger. The things I do for you." He let his cat take him. *Move over, love. Let me have a go at it too.*

Thatch bit the young woman in the belly, on the opposite side of where Maggie had. He could taste the difference in her blood. She was changing. But that didn't mean a hill of beans toward whether she lived or not. That was a different can of worms altogether.

They both stayed with her, dressed now, until the ambulance came that he'd called. The girl was better, but her burns would be there until she had a chance to shift. Thatch knew that she could still die—her wounds were horrific and extensive—but they'd helped her and that was all he could do right now.

Thinking of his oldest, he reached out to him to tell him what they'd done for her. *She saved all the Conrads, son. Every last one of them. And you should know that it was at great risk to her life. Had we not changed her when we did, she'd have died, and that would have been a terrible shame.* Thatcher told him that they were on standby at the hospital, waiting for the first of them to come in. *I can tell you now what's what. The man — someone shot him in the shoulder, and it isn't too far from his heart. Couple of more inches and he'd be a goner. The missus, she has a broken leg, a lot of cuts and such, but is fine as rain other than that.*

And the children? Are they all right? He told his son that the boy had a broken leg and a lot of burns, but not nearly as bad as it could have been. *And the babies? Dad, I delivered those two. I don't want anything to happen to any of them, but those little girls are special.*

Yes, they're good. A little upset with all the hoopla, but fine. Got one of them sucker things in their mouths, but they're not hurt at all. The woman, she's in bad shape, Thatcher. I don't believe she's gonna make it even with what your mom and I did for her. And it was your momma that did it. She was bound and determined that Rogen — that's her name, by the way — wouldn't die. He asked him why someone would do what Rogen had done. *I don't know, but she surely saved those people. And the only way we're going to find out about it is if she lives. I hope she does. I really do, son.*

When she gets here, I promise you that I'll do everything I can to make that happen. I want answers too. Like why would someone, a stranger to the town even, risk their life on a family that she more than likely didn't know? Thatch said he didn't know, but he was glad that she had. *I am as well. All right, Dad. I'll talk to you in a bit. You and Mom coming in?*

Yes. We're going to come in the ambulance with the babies. Help the drivers out a little. They sure are cute little things. Oh, I should contact the alpha. He'll be happy for his pack too. The Conrads, they're good people.

Thatch called the pack leader next. Shane Picket was a good leader—had him a nice sized pack, too. He was a little busy, but said that if he'd hold on a bit, he'd talk to him. Thatch waited on hold while the first group was put into the ambulance. The young woman was first.

"I'm sorry, Thatch. I have a bit of an issue here. I have a family missing." He asked him if it was the Conrads. "Yes. What's happened? You know where they are?"

"Yes, they're on their way to the hospital. Car accident is all I can tell you right now. A young woman, a human, pulled them from the car, it looks like, before it blew. She's in bad shape, the girl is." He asked if he could do anything. "Maggie and I changed her to save her. Right now, Shane, I don't have anything to tell you other than the man had been shot. The woman and the children—thanks, as I said, to the woman—they're all fine."

"Mark was supposed to meet me this morning for a monthly meeting. He's never late. We went by their home and it's been torn apart. Like someone was looking for something. And I'm thinking that they didn't find it from the mess they made leaving." Thatch told him what he knew about the accident and the woman, Rogen. "Rogen Hall? She has a brother too. I can't think of his name right now. They're renting the Parker farm from us. Never seen it look so good.

I'll be going to see him. Jamie, that's this name, Jamie Hall. I'll go by their place and see if I can get him to come with me. They're a very shy couple of kids, if you ask me."

The ambulance was back and they loaded up the man and his wife. She was awake now and asking after her children. Watching her with the kids just made his eyes fill with tears. They were all together now, and it was because of the kindness of a single person. Thatch turned away, blowing his nose, and saw something shiny near the accident.

Asking the police who were all over the scene if he could have that, it more than likely belonged to the girl, Thatch was told he could have it but not to turn it on or anything else right now.

"Surely you don't think that she might have done this." Chief of Police Andrew Keen said he wasn't sure of anything at the moment. "Yes, well, I can see that. It is a mess here."

Andrew asked him again what he'd seen when he came up on the accident. After telling him for the third time, he was allowed to go to the hospital with his wife. They weren't hurt, but perhaps they could help out with the children until the mother was released.

Thatch thought about asking his son if she was going to make it but didn't want to bother him right now. Thatcher was a surgeon, a very good one if anyone asked him. Thatch was proud as a peacock of all his boys, and he'd hurt the man who said anything bad about them.

They had raised them on a dime between them, he liked telling people. Then one day his missus, always the luckiest person he'd ever known, had won the lottery. One of the big ones, as a matter of fact. And they'd been set up for life. They'd even been able to send all the boys to college, as well as put some money away for a rainy day. Jonas, his second to last son, had gone into banking, and had turned that into a nice little investment firm. Not only did he take their money and make a great deal more for them, but he'd been able to make it so the little town profited by it as well.

The hospital was busy, of course. When an accident like this one happened, they all came together to make sure that everyone got the best of care. And their little hospital had been winning awards because of their good work up until a few years ago. Now they'd be lucky if they were able to stay open the way things were going. Most of it still being open was due to his boys; both Thatcher and Dawson worked there and kept it up.

Dawson was his youngest and was an emergency room doctor that specialized in trauma. Thatch wasn't sure what that meant—all the things that brought you to the hospital, he thought, were considered trauma—but he kept that to himself. He didn't want to sound foolish to anyone with such smart children.

Dawson was working on the woman. She was giving him a hard time about keeping her from the children, and he laughed when Dawson did. Mrs. Conrad had been Dawson's teacher's aide in grade school when she'd been fresh out of college.

"I'm going to have to keep you all overnight. You know that, don't you, Mrs. Conrad? I can't let you go home and find out you might have gotten a little more bumped around than it looks like. And the police want to talk to you." She asked about her husband. "He's in surgery to remove the bullet, but he should be fine too."

"I haven't any idea what might have happened, Dawson. We were driving along and then there was something popping around us. Then Mark fell forward. After that, it was a blur of things going on." Dawson didn't say anything about the woman who rescued them, he noticed, and wondered at that. More than likely the staff had been told not to say anything until the family remembered. He was still playing with the baby when Thatcher spoke to him.

Dad, she's out of surgery, but I'm going to pop in and see how Dan is doing in the other room. He won't need me, but I'm going to check anyway. He asked about the woman. *I don't know. I've done about all I could for her. She's going to need skin grafts as well as lots of care. You were right to warn me about how bad it was. It was the only thing that kept me upright when I saw her. Damn, I hurt for her.*

She more than likely would have done it again too, I'm betting. They're all safe, the Conrads. And Shane, he knows her brother, and he was going to go by there and talk to him. I don't know the situation there, but they're renting the old Parker farm. You remember that place, don't you, son? Thatcher said that he did. *It was a sore spot for a long time. I surely hope they're not paying that much.*

I haven't been by there in twenty years. But I'll be down in a few minutes. I want to check on my patient. Dan has finished up with Mr. Conrad, and he's going to recovery now.

Thatch told Mrs. Conrad, and she seemed so relieved that he hugged her when she started crying.

Taking the baby out to the lobby, he was told that someone from the pack was coming for the children. Levi, their brother, was going to have to stay overnight. His burns weren't that bad, but he had broken his leg.

Thatcher came down about an hour after the babies left, and he looked a little worse for wear.

"Son?" Thatcher waved him off, and he wondered what had happened. Thatch just knew that Rogen had died, and he was having a hard time thinking of how to tell him. "It's all right, son. She did a good thing, and she surely helped a lot of people. I'll tell her brother for her so that—"

"She's not dead, Dad. I told you, she's in recovery." He looked around like he was afraid of being overheard. In a harsh whisper, he told him what he'd discovered. "She's my mate. You and Mom, you saved my mate for me."

Thatch was still standing there when Maggie came to get him. He was sure that he'd heard his son wrong. Or he'd heard what he wanted to hear. Maggie was forever telling him that's how he heard things.

"What's the matter, you old fool? You look like you've seen a ghost." Thatch wondered if he should tell her when he realized that he needed to tell her. "Thatch, something happen to that young woman? Please tell me she's going to be all right."

"She is now, I'd say. I think I heard Thatcher say she was his mate." She did the same thing he had—stood there with her mouth gaping open like a fish ready for a fat worm. After closing her mouth, he took her hand so that they could have a seat. And just then, he saw Shane.

"Where is my sister?" The young man with him was screaming about his sister, and that's when Thatch realized this was Rogen's brother. "Someone tell me where I can find my sister! They said she's been hurt."

He made his way to the younger man and got his attention. Before he could ask again where Rogen was, Thatch took him to where he had left Maggie. Jamie, he'd heard his name was, just asked again where she was.

"Recovery. My son, he works here, he worked on her. She's been burned badly." Jamie started crying, and he looked over at Maggie. He didn't know what else to say to Jamie, but Maggie thankfully did.

"She's doing all right now, son. And as soon as they let us, we'll go up and see her. She saved the lives of an entire family." The police were coming toward them when Maggie spoke again. "Now, you help these nice policemen out, and when they're done with their questions, I'll take you up to the surgery floor myself. All right then?"

"Rogen is all I got in the world. We only have each other now." Thatch wanted to tell him that wasn't true anymore but didn't. He wanted to wait on Thatcher to tell them. "Our parents are gone. Dead. We came here for a fresh start. To keep the newspaper people from hounding us again."

Thatch didn't know what that meant but didn't get a chance to ask. Andrew, the chief of police, was asking him about Rogen and her habits. As much as Thatch wanted to stay and listen, he needed to find his son. Thatch needed to confirm what he'd heard from his boy. And if she really was his mate, then he was surely glad that Maggie had started what she'd done for Rogen.

Chapter 2

Jamie watched his sister breathing. He couldn't see her face; they had her on a bed that would move up and down, and a hole where her face was. She was breathing, but she looked really sore. The doctor came in and Jamie stood up. He did it every time the man came in and he knew it was getting on his nerves, but he could no more not do it than breathe.

"What can you tell me about your sister?" Jamie looked at her. They'd said that she might die, and he didn't know what he'd do without her. "Jamie? What can you tell me about her?"

"She's good to me. Never yells unless she's had a bad day." Jamie looked at the big man, and when he sat down, so did Jamie. "I'm not right in the head. I'm not allowed to say that I'm slow — Rogen gets upset with me when I say that — but I'm slow in things."

"What happened that made you like you are? I'm assuming that you've not always been this way." Jamie shook his head and smiled, but let it go almost as soon as he realized that he'd done it. "You're very smart. I can tell that someone has taken the time to help you. Was it your sister?"

"Yes. When I was a little boy, my mom—she didn't like me—she tried to strangle me. I was two. And when I died, Rogen brought me back by pushing hard on my chest. But it was too late for my noddle. That's what Rogen calls it. I love her, you know." The doctor said that he could tell. "My mom and dad were so mad that I came back not right. Slow. I didn't have enough air to my noddle, and that made my thinking slower."

"And Rogen, she's been taking care of you since then? Is she older than you or younger?" He said she was two years older. "So a four year old did CPR on you and brought you back?"

"Rogen, she's really smart. She tells me that she is off the charts. I'm not really sure what that means, but she can do anything she sets her mind to. But she don't...doesn't remember little things well. She said her mind is too busy on other stuff to make the little things work. Like phone numbers and grocery lists. But she can talk in a lot of other words, languages. She works for the government on some computer stuff. I don't know what it is, but she works really hard." The doctor told him to call him Thatcher. "I can't do that. I can't do that until Rogen says it's okay. I'm too trusting, she told me, and I don't do anything without her saying it's okay. It's why I can't let her die. I don't know what I'm to do."

"She'll be all right. I promise you." Jamie looked at his sister, then back at Thatcher. "You know what a shifter is? Like a man that can change?"

"Yes. The man that rents us the house, he is a wolf. But I don't know how to tell what people are. Only the nice ones from the bad." He looked at Rogen again. "You're a shifter thing, aren't you? That's why you know she's going to be all right."

"Yes, I'm a tiger. Bengal. And when my parents, who are both tigers too, came upon the accident where your sister was, they changed her into a tiger to save her life." Thatcher asked him to look at him, and Jamie had to work hard at looking him in the eye. "Jamie, they changed her into a tiger, and she's my mate, my other half. Do you understand that?"

"Yes." Jamie started crying when he realized that this man would own his sister and make her do things she'd not want to. "If you send me away, I won't see her again. I need Rogen. And if you beat her, she will die anyway. Please, I don't know what I can do for you, but please don't send me away and kill her spirit."

"I'd never do that." Jamie didn't believe him. "Jamie, I won't hurt her. Ever. She will never hurt again if I can help it. Did someone tell you that? That I'd beat her?"

"We had neighbors that were bears. They were mean and would scare me all the time by chasing me around the town. And when they'd catch me, they'd hurt me with their claws, and I'd have to have the hospital fix me up. Rogen told them that if they did it again, that she'd kill them. I believed her, but I don't think they did." Thatcher asked him what had happened. "One night they were trying to get me to run, but I'd been sick with the flu. Rogen heard them and came out of her room with a gun and shot the biggest one. She even put a special bullet in the gun to make it hurt bad. The man died, and she didn't go to jail because they were in the house. Mom and Dad, they were so angry that they beat her up bad."

"That's not right. You know that, don't you? Where are your parents, Jamie?" He looked at Rogen, then back at the man again. "You can't tell me?"

"I'm suppose to tell everyone that they're dead." Thatcher seemed to get it and nodded. "You won't tell on me, will you?

Rogen won't be mad at me, but she might not bake cookies for me. She makes the best chocolate chip in the world."

"I won't tell her." Jamie thanked him. "You thought that I'd send you away. I'm assuming that this is from your parents as well?"

"Yes. They said that nobody would want a...." He lowered his voice to a whisper. "They'd not want a retard around all the time. And if you didn't get to send me away, then you'd beat Rogen until she said okay."

"You have a home with us as long as you want." He nodded. "Jamie, I'm not just saying that. I swear to you on the life of my parents that I'd never send you away. You are my brother, just the same as Rogen is your sister."

He cried again. Jamie knew that he was too emotional sometimes. It was all he could do not to hug the big man. But he stayed where he was, thankful that someone wasn't going to hurt him or Rogen. At least that was what he was saying now.

"I have to help your sister's wounds. And to do that, I need to change into my tiger. My mouth has healing powers in it that will keep her from getting an infection, and the sores will go away much faster. You can stay if you'd like, or you can wait in the hall. But I have to do this daily in order for her to get better." He asked if he'd bite him. "No. Not unless you want me to. Do you?"

"No thank you." Thatcher laughed and stood up. "I think I'd like to stay. If you really don't mind."

"No. You should get used to the tigers anyway. But don't allow anyone to come in with us, all right? I have to take some of the bandages off her skin so that I can get to it as a tiger." He looked at Rogen as he continued telling him what he was going to do. "I'm going to lick the worst of them, then I'm going to nip at her skin again, just to give her a part of myself she needs."

"Rogen told me a long time ago that you could be able to talk to me if you took my blood. Can that help too?" Thatcher said that he'd have to bite him gently as a tiger. "If it helps my sister, then I'll do it. But not too hard. Okay? I'm a big baby."

"No, you're a good man who loves his sister. And I thank you for that." Touched, Jamie waited in the seat while Thatcher went into the bathroom. "I won't be long now."

Jamie was careful when the big tiger came out of the bathroom. He was huge, his head about to Jamie's when he was seated. And when he laid his head on his lap, Jamie reached out his hand slowly, just to touch the pretty fur.

"You're very soft, aren't you? Like a stuffed animal." He petted him more and smiled at him. "I know you have big teeth, but when you bite me, please only use the little ones."

Jamie put out his hand, but it was shaking a lot, so he was embarrassed. The huge tongue that licked his hand was rough, like sandpaper that he used when he had projects to do. Thatcher bit him and it wasn't so bad, and then he licked away the blood. The wound was gone except for a little scar on his hand.

Hello. Jamie laughed out loud, something he rarely did. *I forgot to lock the door. Can you do that for me? Then I'll get started.*

When he turned back after locking the door, the big tiger was up on the bed and licking at the wounds on Rogen's back. There were a lot of them. And big blisters too. Jamie's heart hurt for her, and he walked closer to the bed to touch the big tiger.

"When I was ten, my mom wanted to send me away. She kept telling me I was worthless every time I saw her." The purring of the big animal calmed him in ways that he'd never had before. "She killed cats all over town, telling people that I'd done it. Then dogs when that didn't work. Rogen caught her doing it by recording it on her cell phone. Then everybody didn't like Mom anymore. She had to pay money to everyone that she'd hurt that way. Then when Rogen was going to college, my dad tied me the tree out back all day while she was gone."

I'm sorry about that, Jamie. No one should treat their child that way. He nodded and moved back when Thatcher moved off the bed to stand near Rogen's legs. *Can you pull the sheet away for me? I can do her legs this way too.*

"Rogen came home early because her class was canceled because of the snow. And when she found me there, she was very angry. And it scared me what she might do." Thatcher moved away from the bed a little and bit down on Rogen's leg. "She'll be better soon, won't she?"

Yes. What did your sister do to your parents? And how old were you? He told him how old he was. *Your sister was in college at twelve? That's impressive. She must really be smart.*

"She is. When she figured out that they'd been doing that to me all along—I wasn't allowed to tell her—she had a hissy fit." He so loved that word, hissy. "She didn't do anything to them then. She said that one more day and she'd have them. I didn't know what she meant, but the very next day, she went to college and told me that I'd be safe after that. I was really sad for her. It looked like she hurt all the way to her toes."

Thatcher asked if he could change before he told him the rest. Nodding, he sat back down on the chair, thinking that he'd never felt this safe with anyone but Rogen. And when Thatcher came out of the bathroom, dressed like he was before, Jamie couldn't help himself. He hugged the big man and cried again when he hugged him back.

"She made it so everyone could see it. I don't know what it was, but people would come by and throw things at the house. The police came and came, and then took me away. Rogen had to visit me in a place that I hated. It was forever before she came to get me, but I was free at last. Then we came here. She said that we'd be safe." Jamie looked at Thatcher and could see his pretty cat in his eyes. "You won't let them hurt her again, will you? She doesn't like people anymore, and we came here to start over. Help her start over, will you, Thatcher? Please. I don't want her hurt again."

"She won't be. I promise you. And if they come here, they'll be sorry as hell that they fucked around with the wrong family."

Jamie was twenty-seven years old and he had his first friend, he was sure of it. And he believed that if anyone could keep her from being hurt again, it would be this giant, gentle man.

After hugging him, Thatcher invited him to lunch with him. "I'm off duty until tomorrow, and I thought it would be nice if you got to know my family. And I'd like it if you come and stay at my house. You'll be safer there." He told him that he had to watch over Rogen's plants and computers. "We can bring it all to my house too, if that will be all right with you. I'm worried now, you see. The newspaper has put out an article about how Rogen saved all those people. It might just bring your parents here."

"No." Jamie felt his body tense up, his heart pounding in his chest. "They'll hurt us. They'll come for me and hurt us."

"They won't. Not if you allow me to keep you safe." He wanted to be safe. Jamie wanted his sister to be safe. Nodding, he thought it was a good idea if her things were safe too. Rogen loved her plants, and the computer, he'd been told, was special. "All right, I'll have it moved over today. And her plants. All right?"

"Yes, all right. But no matter what, you have to keep Rogen safe from them. They don't like her. and they will hurt her bad." He promised that he would. "Okay. You can move us. I have stuff too, but I can leave it there. It's my projects."

"I can get you completely moved to my home, Jamie. Including your projects. You come with me to my parents' house, and then we'll work on getting it all moved from there."

Jamie wasn't sure that Rogen was going to like anyone messing with her computer, but they'd be safe, and she told him all the time that he was able to make big decisions on his own. And he did this time. He only hoped he wasn't too trusting, like Rogen said he could be.

~*~

"Thatcher, you might want to have Jonas come and take this stuff to your home." He asked him why he couldn't do it. "Because I have a feeling that if I unhook any one of the things she has hooked up in there, I'm going to go before a firing squad. And that's before your new mate touches me. Come look."

"Holy shit." There were eight large monitors mounted on the walls, each one of them with a different scene going on somewhere. It wasn't all the United States, he could tell that, but from all around the world. There were different computers too, each with their own monitor, mouse, and keyboard. "I wonder what she does, and if she's on our side."

"She is." They both turned around and looked at the men there. The man who spoke, a well-dressed gentlemen, asked if they'd come out of her room. "She's working for the US government. And we've been unable to contact her for some time now. Why are you here, Dr. Robinson?"

"You know me." The man nodded. "Are you going to give me your name as well? And for that matter, let my brothers go?"

Each of them were on the floor with a gun to their head. The men standing over them were dressed for war. All but their eyes were covered, and they did not look like they'd stop at anything unless given the command.

"They're all right where they are. And before you let that beast of yours go, you should know that each of the men behind me have silver in their rifles. And they will not hesitate to use them." The man sat down on the couch and pointed to the chairs across from him. "This will go so much better if you cooperate, Dr. Robinson."

Thatcher sat, but he wasn't happy about it. "I'm assuming that you know that Rogen is in the hospital. What you might not know or care about is that she's my mate." That surprised the man, but if Thatcher hadn't been looking right at him, he would have missed it. Glancing out the window, he saw something that the man might not be aware of. "If your men do not let my brothers go, then you'll leave me no choice but to protect what is mine."

"You think so, do you?"

The breaking of glass and screams was heard a split second later. The man, now with a large wolf at his throat, was down on the couch and his men were all down as well, each of them with a large pissed off tiger on their chest.

"While I'm sure that it will take some effort on their part, I'm positive that those cats can tear though their body armor in seconds. And they will tear their throats out with only a small signal from me. Also, the wolves have been joined by my leap, sir, and you'll give me answers or I'll have you in a pit so deep that you'll never see the light of day again."

"I had to see. If you could protect her on your own. I should have— Christ, he's cutting into my neck." Thatcher didn't ask Shane to let him go; he still had no answers. "I didn't know that she was your mate. If I had, I might—I would have done this differently. Can I be released now?"

"Not just yet. Who are you?" Agent Donaldson had bitten off a bit more than he could chew, it seemed. "And my mate, she works for you?"

"I'm her direct contact. She actually works for you and everyone else in the United States. If you'd allow me to get up, I can show you a few things." Thatcher said that if he reached for a gun, he was personally going to rip his arm off. "You're very violent, aren't you? I have to say; you and Rogen will get along splendidly. By the way, you will see more staff at the hospital. They're there for her protection as well as yours. Rogen Hall is very important to a great many people. And when she came up missing, it took us several days to find her."

"We didn't think it would be good for her or her brother to put out there where she was. But the paper put out an article before I could ask them not to." Agent Donaldson sat up and reached very slowly into his jacket pocket. "Just so we're clear on something. You come back here like this again, and I won't wait for the wolf pack to come and distract you. I will kill you. Simple as that."

"I was wrong about you. I know you and Rogen will get along just fine. She's a lot like you. Strong, pig headed. A little on the scary side." He handed him a thumb drive. "That's the aero shot of what happened that day, if you'd like to see it. When I did, I was first sickened at her pain, and then pissed at her stupidity. But she saved them all, as you know, at the risk of getting herself killed. And you will want the pack leader to know that a man is out to kill his pack, one family at a time. Here is the plate number that we took off of Rogen's cell phone that morning."

"And you want me to put this in one of those computers in there, like there might not be a virus on them." He said that he'd have to learn to trust him sooner or later. "I don't right now. And that's the point, I think. I don't know you from anyone."

Thatcher's cell phone rang, along with all his brothers' phones that were scattered all around the floor. He didn't know what was going on, but he thought that the man in front of him had a great deal to do with it. When Donaldson suggested that he answer it, Thatcher did.

"Hello, Thatcher. My name is Winnie James. Mr. Donaldson works directly with me and the president. If you would be so kind as to do as he asks, I won't have to send in the bigger boys to make you. I've had a really long day, and as you can imagine, you're fucking with my day even more." Thatcher laughed. "Yes, well, you won't think I'm so funny if I have to come there, sir."

"Did you catch that Rogen is my mate?" She asked him to hang on, and that's when Donaldson's phone rang. "I don't think she's going to be any happier with you than she is me at the moment."

Thatcher could hear the woman talking to Donaldson. She wasn't loud, but she was pissed off. And about every other word that came out of her mouth was a four letter or more word that didn't bode well for the man. When he put the phone down, he handed him the thumb drive.

"Thatcher, could you pretty please with sugar on top put the thumb drive in?"

Thatcher laughed and could hear his brothers doing the same thing. It wasn't until he stood up that the men on the floor were released. Taking the drive into the large room, he pushed it into one of the computers. It was Rogen, running in a bright green running suit and reflective shoes.

"As you can see, we know where she is at all times. This is routine for her, an early morning run. I can't get her to stop it, or at least go at a different time; she refuses. Something about waking the sun up." Thatcher looked at the man as Rogen, the one he'd never seen before, ran down the darkened street. "I suppose you understand."

"Yes. She likes the time between the darkness and the sun rising. I don't run, but I do watch it come up, cresting over the hill wherever I am." He looked back at the screen. "You have a camera on her at all times? Isn't that sort of routine for you as well?"

"I suppose. Next, you'll see the car go by. She might not know the family, but I went back and looked. She sees them just about in this same spot every day through the week. Waving at the young man in the back seat." He told him his name. "We knew the family only by this, but we know them all now. You can see the accident occur, but not well. We were looking at her, not the car."

He saw it then. The smoke, the skidding car, and the other one racing off. Donaldson asked him if he knew the car. Thatcher said that he didn't, but he might know the person if he could see him.

"You can't. We tried to get a better shot of him, but he's very clever. He's the one that caused the initial accident. Watch her come up on the scene."

The video came into crystal clear focus, like he was right there with her. Rogen ran to the car, and he could see how she got the husband out, then the wife. The point where she messaged herself the plate number. All the time she worked, Thatcher could see every pain that she had each time she was burnt again. The babies were taken out one at a time, their little bodies clinging to Rogen's. Thatcher could almost hear them screaming, their cries breaking the morning quietness. Then when the car came back, throwing what looked like a Molotov cocktail into the burning car, Thatcher wanted to go there and grab her when she started flying backward with Levi in her arms.

"She literally did save their lives. Do you think the would-be killer would have known she was there?" Donaldson said that he didn't think so but wasn't going to take any chances. "Neither will I."

"We're playing right now on the assumption that he wanted the pack member dead, as well as his family. Since we can't ask the 'would-be killer,' as you called him, yet, we have to be careful who knows the entire story here." Thatcher asked him why the papers put out that she was a hero. "Yes, but that's all they know. If you'll notice, the paper doesn't say that she lives in this town. Nor that she has any family members. She was just a person, Rogen Hall, that was out for a run and happened upon them. Basically, this is true, but we don't want anyone to come for her."

"Her parents." Donaldson asked him how he knew about him. "Rogen's brother. Jamie. I talked to him. He's terrified of his parents that may or may not be coming for them. His words, they don't like him."

"Wait. Rogen has a brother?"

Chapter 3

Rogen was sure that she was dead. All she could see was white. And she felt odd, like there was something moving over her skin. When a pair of clean white tennis shoes were in her vision, she listened while the man talked, presumably to himself.

"Why they have to do this today is beyond me. Stupid asses. I would like for someone to say, just once 'Hey Dawson, thanks for doing a good job. Would you mind going in to help your brother out? He seems to have disappeared off the face of the fucking earth.' I know just where he is, and I'm going to—"

"I don't think I'm dead, am I? I mean, hell might sound like this, but I don't think I've been that bad. And angels would not, I don't believe, curse like that. Do you think?" The shoes jumped out of her vision and she waited. "I don't know who you are, Dawson, but I thank you for doing a good job. Unless you're here trying to kill me; then, sorry, no kudos from me."

His face suddenly appeared in front of her face. He was

bent at such an odd angle that she was reasonably sure that he was very tall. Dawson had a smile that would win him any argument, she thought, and never leave him without a bed partner.

"No, not trying to kill you, my dear. But to keep someone from giving you too much in the way of fluids. You're supposed to be getting off them a little at a time. I'm Dawson Robinson. Doctor. But you can call me Dawson."

"Rogen Hall. Where am I?" He told her she was in the burn unit of the local hospital. "Burn unit? Oh, the family. Are they all right? Did anyone get them help? I'm so very sorry that the little boy was burnt, but I did try my best to—"

What's the matter? She looked at Dawson and realized that it wasn't him that was talking to her. *Rogen, I'm in a meeting about you and your job. Can you tell me if you're all right?*

"Hmm. Dawson, there's a man talking to me in my head. Perhaps I did die?" Dawson laughed and said it was Thatcher. "And this Thatcher person, does he go around talking to strangers?"

"No. Normally, no. But he did make it so you could talk to him. He's talking to me now and would very much like for you to answer him." She asked him how she was to do that. "Just think of...no, that won't work. Just think of answering him and you can. Just think up your answer and he'll hear it." Well, she had a few things to say to this Thatcher person. And damn it, she was going to.

Who are you, and what the hell does your brother mean, you "fixed it so I could talk to you"? You fucking bastard, if you've planted something in my head or my ear, so help me, I'll find you. And you can go to the bank on that. His laughter caught her off guard in her rant. It was just too sexy and nice. *Who the fuck are you?*

Thatcher Robinson. Dawson, who you've met, is my brother. We're both doctors. You are my patient, and since I couldn't be there to check up on your dosage of fluids, he said he'd do it for me. She told Thatcher that he should thank his brother more often. *I do. I think he's talking about the head of the hospital. He's a mean prick that has risen above his level of competency.*

Rogen thought of the people she knew who had done that. Risen up into a position of authority but didn't have the first clue on what they were doing. Other than pissing people off and fucking up her day.

Those people that were in the car. Did they all get well? I mean, the man was shot, and the little boy was hurt badly when I was too long in getting him out of the car. He didn't say anything. Then it occurred to her what he'd said he was doing. *You said you were in a meeting about me. Why?*

I've come in contact with your boss, Donaldson. There's another shit head that has gone above his level of competency. Anyway, he was getting a hard time from me – not that he didn't deserve it – but then Winnie James stepped in. She's scary, isn't she? Rogen told Thatcher that she'd trained Winnie. *I can see that, I suppose. You're supposed to be very scary too, aren't you? And you do a hell of a job for the country.*

She felt her body flush with embarrassment. Rogen didn't do well with praise. She supposed it was because she seldom received it and had no idea how to react. And most of the time, if not always, it wasn't sincere, just something that was said to someone. But this man, for some reason, made her feel like he meant it. Every word.

I would like to get out of this contraption. Is that even remotely possible? And I have a brother, Jamie. I have to see to him. He told her that Jamie was with his parents, learning how to cook, and the contraption would have to wait until she saw him again.

And if I just leave? What will you do then, Mr. Bigshot Doctor?

Well, I'd like to think that you're a reasonable person, and will wait until you're released so as you don't get an infection in those burns. She'd forgotten about the burns. The pain of them. Her heart started to race—her breathing wasn't right. It wasn't until she was ready to pass out that she heard the voice in her head and the one in front of her. *Just calm down. Breathe. Or Dawson is going to have a heart attack. Breath for me, Rogen. Close your eyes and think of a place that calms you.*

The first thing that popped into her head was a big bed, silky sheets, and a man that filled the bed up, and her. When she heard his sexy laughter again, she thought of other things. This man tied up, his arms and legs spread out so that— She could almost see him naked, his body hard for her.

You have to stop that, love, or I'm not going to be able to leave this meeting without a large box in front of my cock. Embarrassed again, she didn't want to talk to him. *I'll be there soon. I think they've told me about all they're going to. And I suppose, if you're willing, you can give me the rest. Are you all right?*

Yes. Why wouldn't I be? And that wasn't you I was thinking of. It was someone else. From a long time ago. Not you. He told her that she was still a virgin. *How do you know what I am?*

I could taste it. She had no idea what to say to that, so didn't comment. *I'll be there in about a half hour. Talk to Dawson, love. He has all the information you might need on the family. But trust me, you saved their lives, and the entire pack is grateful to you.*

"Thatcher said that I should talk to you." He raised her up by pushing a button, putting her face level with his after he sat down. "What is this thing? Some sort of rotating bed?"

"Something like that. Since you can't be rolled to your back because of the burns, we have you on this rotating bed that can flip you over or stand you up, like you are now, to keep the blood circulating. If you notice, your feet are on a platform so that you can stand and get blood to your feet and legs." She thanked him. "No problem. What else did you want to know? And whatever you ask me, you must know that I cannot lie to you. Not even a white lie. All right?"

"Why? Why is it that you can't lie to me?" He looked away, then back at her. "This is something that your brother has to tell me, correct?"

"Yes and no. I can tell you that he's healed you. And since I'm sure you're aware of what a shifter is, I'll tell you that we're all cats. Tigers, as a matter of fact."

She nodded, then got what he was telling her. "Oh no. No, no, no, no. I am not his mate." Dawson laughed and said that she was brilliant. "Brilliant or not, I am not going to be a slave to any man. And I won't be sending my brother away, nor will I quit my job to wait on his fucking ass hand and foot. He's in for a huge awakening if he thinks I'm a pushover."

"I don't think anyone would ever think that you're a pushover, Rogen." She told him she was sorry. "No reason to be sorry. I like you. And your brother. I've talked to Jamie. He's a nice young man, by the way, and is very happy that you're going to be all right. He told me about your experiences with shifters—the neighbors of yours. We're not like that. First of all, Mom would beat us to death, literally. And second, you would too. And to be honest with you, Rogen, I'm terrified of both of you."

"I'm not much of a fighter, Dawson." Something moved over her, and she closed her eyes. There it was. A tiger. Opening her eyes, she looked at Dawson. "I'm a cat. That's how I survived this, isn't it? That man, Thatcher, he changed me to keep me in line. I won't have it—"

"My parents changed you. Out there on the road before

anyone knew what you were to Thatcher. And while I like you, Rogen, very much, you really need to take it down a few notches. No one is out to get you. There is not one person in our family that will harm you. And most of all, Thatcher is the nicest and most generous person I know." He stood up. "If you would just get that chip off your shoulder for one moment, you'd realized that the only reason that you're alive and healed, for the most part, is because my family stepped in and saved you."

Rogen started crying. She wasn't normally this emotional all the time, but the last few...well, she had no idea how long it had been. But she rarely cried, and she wasn't snippy. She'd have to apologize to a great many people if she kept this up. And when a man came in, she knew that he had to be Thatcher.

"I'm sorry that Dawson upset you." She said that he hadn't. Just told the truth. "Yes, well, he can be too blunt at times. How are you feeling?"

"Emotionally drained. I think I insulted your entire lineage. Not to mention upset your brother and a nurse from last night. She startled me, and I had no idea where I was." He sat down. "Am I to assume that you're the famed Thatcher Robinson, my mate?"

"Your temper is showing again. And yes, to both. Do you have a problem with being my mate, or is it just me?" She told him both. "So, you don't have a problem with me, just with being a mate to anyone in general."

"I know that Dawson, who looks a great deal like you, by the way, he said that I'd been wrong about mates. But I saw it firsthand what being a slave to someone is like." He asked her if she wanted to get out of her contraption now. "Don't do that. Don't fob me off like a child when you don't think I can handle the answer."

"I'm not. I'm simply asking you if you'd like to stand on your own two feet. Dawson said that you were doing well enough, he thought, and when I came in, I saw that you're nearly healed. Would you like to get out of the bed?" She nodded, not sure at all what was wrong with her. Thatcher moved behind her and she could feel him working on something that was holding her. "You know you're a cat, but I would suggest you hold off for at least two days before shifting. You're very weak, and she will be as well."

The pressure at her back was let go, but Thatcher held her in place while he did something right around her butt. When she felt it give, she had to hold onto the bed before falling all the way back. She really was weak.

"Come on now, you can do this. Just breathe." She wondered why he kept saying that to her when she realized she wasn't breathing. Rogen let her breath out slowly. "That's my girl. In and out. Just like you do every day. You're doing well, and if you want to take a step back you can. But it's about a six or seven inch difference from the bed to the floor."

The step was taken, but she was shaky and weak. Before she could begin to think she should get back on the contraption, Thatcher picked her up in his arms and sat her down on the chair he'd been in. She wasn't sure if she should be grateful or embarrassed.

"How long have I been here?" He told her. "Not that long at all, is it? For how badly I was burnt. You said that you talked to Donaldson. He's an ass kisser, and he follows the rules like they were something that God handed down to him. I don't. Follow rules, I mean. That's why I'm so good at what I do."

"What is it you do? They might have told me at the meeting, but I missed it when you were upset." She apologized to him.

"No need to do that. You were upset, and that's normal when you wake up after what you went through. They said that you can make a computer do whatever you wish, and if you can't then you just make up a new program for it to dance for you."

"Yes. I guess. I'm the person who finds the people the government wants me to find. I don't ask for what. I just do it." She adjusted on the seat, her back hurting just a little. "I find that I can sleep better at nights if I only think they want something from them. Not that they're going to kill them."

"You're my mate, Rogen. You know that. But I am never going to tell you not to do your job. It's obviously something that you're good at and seem to enjoy." She nodded. "But we have to talk about your parents. I'm concerned that they might be on their way here."

~*~

Thatcher wanted to take her home and let her shift. He wanted to kiss her, make love to her, and tell her how much he admired her. But he'd been cautioned by Winnie not to go too fast. And never to pay her a compliment that was not sincere. She could tell it wasn't at the first word. Now that was a woman that he liked.

Donaldson hadn't done anything to him. Not really. Nor had he been a total ass like he had been on their first meeting. But he was a dick, and he let everyone around him know that he was in charge for a reason. What that reason might have been, no one seemed to know.

"For the most part, everyone comes to me after talking with Donaldson. The only people that have contact with Rogen are me and that idiot that she reports to. And so you know, Rogen blind copies me on every email that she sends him." He asked why he'd need to know that. "Because, if you have to email me, like if I need to know if Rogen is ill or hurt, I'd like it if you'd do the same. You have no idea how many times I've had to step in when he has this thing he wants done. I have to admit, Rogen handles him like we all wish we could. She tells him to fuck off, shut up, and to get the hell away from her when he's being a bore. Me, I have to watch myself, but that's getting harder and harder to do daily."

Rogen stood up, taking him out of his musings. "Are you all right? I mean, other than a little shaky?"

"No. I mean, shaky, yes, but...I'm confused right now. And I feel antsy. I'm assuming that is the cat. I can see her when I close my eyes, but she's far back, like she's afraid of me. But when your brother was here, or when I was being pissy to you, she seemed to run over me, like a hug. But that can't be right, can it?"

Thatcher told her what he knew. "I guess that's as good a description as any. Giving you a hug to let you know that she's here for you should you need her. And she's more than likely back from you because she knows that as long as I'm here with you, she's not needed." Rogen glared at him. "I don't mean that you're the weak female. It's just that she knows that you've been hurt, and right now, without being able to shift, she doesn't need to protect you like she normally would."

She didn't so much pace the floor as she lightly glided from one end of the room to the other. He'd seen his dad pace. It was like he was trying to make a hole in the carpet while he thought about things. When she stopped moving, he looked up at her face. She had such a beautiful one too.

"Your parents, what does me being changed by them mean?" Thatcher asked her what she meant. "Well, when a vampire changes you, they own you or something. At least that's what I heard. What does me being changed by them mean?"

"Nothing. They changed you because you needed it. The council, the tiger board, they understood and are glad that they were able to save you. For me." Rogen didn't say anything about that, but she did ask what would have happened had they not approved. "I don't know, honestly. You're the first person that any of us has been around that we had a hand in changing. And when I say we, I mean me as well. Every day when I could, I'd come in and nip at your skin. Just enough to draw blood and for my salvia to mix with it. It's what healed you so quickly."

"So you could have sex with me." She was trying to pick a fight with him. He wasn't sure why, but he wasn't going to let her get to him. He'd heard enough from Winnie to know that she trusted no one, not even her, and that bothered the other woman. "Is that it? You healed me so that you could fuck me anytime you wanted and order me around?"

"Do I look like a person that would order you around? Have I given you any indication that I'd knock you on your ass?" Her face turned pink. "While I do have some idea why you're this way, I'm not the bad guy in all this. All I've done since I've found you, or since you were brought to me, is try and make you safer and well. Perhaps I should go home and let you cool off."

"I don't know what's wrong with me." She started crying, and his cat seemed to want to come out and be there for her. When she looked at him, he had to hold onto his cat so he didn't do just what he wanted. "Can I go home? I can't be here anymore. It's too noisy. Too much going on. And now it seems as if I can smell every kind of floor polish they used here."

"All right. But you don't live in the rental anymore." She started to get angry again, but he held up his hand. "Even Donaldson said you weren't safe there. It's too far off the beaten path. There isn't anyone around for miles, and you don't own a car or a good cell phone. Those are just a few of the things that were pointed out to me."

"I had a lot of equipment at the rental. I do hope whoever did this, without my permission, did a good job of taking it all down." He told her that his brothers had taken it down with the supervision of Winnie. "How big is this place that I'm living now? I want my brother there too. I need him much more than he needs me."

"He's living with us too." She looked at him. "I can't protect you if you're in another home. And I have enough people, pack and the ambush, right there if you ever need them. Plus, plenty of land surrounding us so that you can run if you wish. And if you want to sleep with me, I'm just down the hall from your room."

"I don't like this." He wisely, he thought, didn't say anything. "I don't have anything to wear home. I'm sure that the things I came in here with aren't wearable either."

"My mom got a few things out of your clothing at your rental. She said that it would be better to get it before it was boxed up rather than after. I think they're in that closet over there." She walked over and bent to get them. He smiled when her bare ass was shown to him. "You might want to remember that you're naked under that gown. It was easier for us to put meds on you when you came in."

Her face was as bright red as he'd ever seen a woman's. She didn't say anything more to him but walked to the bathroom facing him with the gown clutched in her hand in the back. Rogen was adorable. And he could not wait to learn all he could from her.

"I thought that once you got home you could talk to Mrs. Beasley. She's our cook. I'm not home all that much, it seems, and she might be better cooking for you instead of me most nights." She said something, but he didn't know what it was, so he continued. "There is a maid service that comes in daily. And I have a butler that also drives me when I don't want to drive myself. It's a nice perk, but I keep Rankin around more because he's a funny man than because I need him to drive me around. Plus, I think his family could use the extra money."

The door opened, and Thatcher knew right then that his mom was doing this on purpose. The clothing that Rogen had on was a running outfit, skin tight, and the prettiest shade of blue he'd ever seen. Clearing his throat several times, he asked if she was ready to go.

"I don't usually wear this kind of stuff unless I'm running. I was amazed that it didn't hurt my skin when I put it on. It's really tight, isn't it?" All he could manage was a strangled yes. "Now what I have done?"

"Nothing. It's me. All me." Thatcher cleared his throat. "We really should be going if you want to get out of here. I mean, you do, don't you?"

She crossed her arms in front of her, and all it did for him was make his cock harder and his breathing more difficult. He wanted to beg her to stop torturing him, but he knew that would lead to more questions. And right now, Thatcher wasn't sure he had enough blood in his head to even tell her his name.

Instead of getting into any kind of argument, and he knew there would be with her, he left the room. He could tell the moment that she started to follow him, and he knew as soon as they were in the elevator or the car, she was going to start on him again. This time, he told himself, he'd be ready for her. As soon as the doors closed around them, Thatcher reached for her. He was more than happy that she came willingly into his arms.

The kiss wasn't hot, it was volcanic. Her touch was like having a mark with a hot branding iron touching him. Everywhere she touched him, every breath that blew over his face, was more than he could handle, yet not nearly enough. Thatcher wanted it all, right here, right now. If not for the sound of the elevator dinging to signal a floor was being stopped on, he was positive that neither of them would have made it out clothed.

Breathing hard, he pushed her against the wall. It didn't escape his notice that she too had to hold onto the railing. And as soon as the doors opened, Thatcher groaned. It was his brother Beckett. And he knew that he could smell them both.

"Going home?" He nodded at his brother, wanting to knock him on his ass right then. "You might want to find someplace for a few hours. Your home is being invaded by the Feds. I think they're setting up your mate's job."

"I have to be there." He nodded at Rogen. "You don't have to come if you have better things to do."

Beckett burst out laughing, and Thatcher did hit him, but not hard enough to do the damage he wanted to do to him. Beckett was going to pay, Thatcher thought. He didn't know when it would be, but he would surely pay for this.

"I'll take you there and show you around after they're finished up. Winnie said that they'd be there for a few hours anyway. And she also, after looking my house over, said that the basement would be the best place for you. She said it would be expandable for you."

"Yes, thank you." She was embarrassed and he didn't blame her. "I'm sorry. I don't know what came over me."

"We'll talk later, Rogen. There is nothing for you to be sorry for." He looked at Beckett when he apologized as well. "We'll go to our home, look around, and get you set up. I'm to understand that there are some unfinished projects that you have to get to as well."

He drove them to their home, his mind simply doing one thing at a time. Breathe, turn here, keep the speed down. Don't hit a tree. These and other things looped in his mind until he pulled up in front of the house and saw that the Feds really had invaded his home.

Chapter 4

The room was coming along—or she should say rooms. The team had come in and were following her directions without question. And when she looked at Thatcher to get his permission on the installment of a wall, he said so long as it didn't mess with the structure of the house, whatever she did was fine by him. He'd even put her chair together for her.

So far all she'd been able to see of the mammoth house was the basement level. They had even entered the house by the lower level. When she was asked to okay a delivery, Thatcher said he'd take care of it for her, and she hooked up the second in a long line of monitors. Which, she thought, were all new.

When the air-conditioning unit was finished being installed, the man who had put it in, another government worker, showed both her and Thatcher how to keep it at a certain temperature. It was to keep her servers cold, and she hadn't had that before either. Taking Winnie aside while a huge refrigerator was being put in, she asked her what was going on.

"You have someone to keep you safe now. And not only

that, you're in a secure house, not one that you're renting. You have room for all this, as well as more should you need it." She asked about the fridge. "That is all on Thatcher. I told him how you sometimes forget to get food and water when you're working, and he said he'd make it easier on you. I believe there is going to be a bunch of snacks put down here as well that you can munch on."

She didn't like this. Not him knowing her habits, but also the way he was avoiding her, the short answers he was giving her, as well as the fact that she'd catch him staring at her like she was some sort of bug under a microscope or something. Finding him outside with another one of his brothers, she walked up to him and slapped him hard across the face.

"What, may I ask, was that for? If it was for kissing you, you're a little delayed on that." She drew back to hit him again when his brother walked away. "Once was enough if you were only trying to get my attention. What is it, Rogen?"

"Why are you treating me this way? I didn't do anything but kiss you, and now you're acting like I'm some sort of—I don't know, hooker that you've paid off. And now I'm hanging around you and you hate it." Thatcher told her that she wasn't correct. "Then perhaps you can tell me why you're treating me this way. You know, I could just move to my other house. I might not have as much equipment or room, but I'd have my fucking dignity."

He didn't answer her. No, instead he pulled her up off her feet and into his arms. The kiss this time didn't seem to be as tempered as before, like he wasn't holding back, and he had no intentions of every stopping. When he set her down on her feet and stepped back, she wanted to hit him again. But then he spoke through clenched teeth before she could do anything.

"I'm hanging on here by a thread. Your scent, your arousal, is driving me and my cat insane. I want you so badly that I'm tempted to throw you to the ground and have you right now. But I'm holding on so that I don't embarrass you when I have you screaming out your releases so that everyone in this house can hear you." She said oh. "Yes, oh. And you might want to warn your fucking boss that if he doesn't keep his hands off you, I'm going to shift, tear him apart, then eat him for my dinner. I'm a jealous man, and my cat is worse."

With that, he pulled her to him for a fast, hot kiss, then walked away, saying something over his shoulder that sounded like he was taking another cold shower. Rogen wondered how many he'd had and laughed. Before she could catch herself, she was bent over with humor. Thatcher Robinson was frustrated. By her.

Skipping just a little, Rogen went back to the office that was hers. It seemed better now. Bigger too. And it was hers. Going to the monitors again, she started hooking up the next one in line. With the way they were bringing in more and more equipment, she was going to need something more to keep her from being found out.

Rogen paused in her work when she thought about all the things she was going to have to do to keep her place of work quiet. She thought of Thatcher and his family. How, now that she was working in such close quarters to them, they'd be targets as well. She saw Jamie just as she was going to find Winnie.

"There you are. Where have you been hiding yourself." Jamie hugged her for the third time, and she wondered if Thatcher's cat would smell him on her. Rogen would make a list of things that she needed to figure out. She realized she'd missed some of what Jamie was telling her. "I'm sorry. You know me, I zoned out for a moment."

"I got me a place to do my projects too." She asked him if he was working in the garage. "No, I have a big barn that I can work with. Come look at it. You won't believe the things that Thatcher got me. But I can't use some of it unless he shows me how to use it and I'm safe. He's a nice man. You should marry him."

"Marry him? Where on earth did you get something like that from?" He laughed and said he was joking. "You shouldn't say things like that, Jamie. Someone might think that you're serious. But show me your barn. I want to see it."

They were nearly to it when she realized that Thatcher had had this barn built recently. Not only was it brand new, but it also had heat and air conditioning. As soon as she entered, she had to hold onto the chair right inside the door. It was a woodworker's dream shop.

"He told me that this was all mine, and when I sold some of my stuff, I had to only pay him one percent. He even showed me how to figure that out. Isn't this really nice, Rogen? It's so pretty. You have to let me stay here with him. Thatcher is so nice to me." She just looked around. "Look over here. It's my own special place to take a snooze, like you call them. He said that taking a nap isn't for babies. He takes them all the time when he's working too hard. Thatcher told me that being too sleepy can make you hurt someone or yourself, and that taking a power nap will save a life."

"He would know. Thatcher is a doctor." There were stacks of wood, all the different types, put into neat piles with the names of the wood on them. "This is really nice, Jamie. I hope you thanked him."

If he answered her, she didn't know. She was looking at the art that Jamie had already been working on. And he was good at it too. Even with his mind just a little fuzzy on some things, he could take wood and make it into beautiful works of art that he sold all over the world.

"I'll have to get you someone to help you with the labels and money, you know." Jamie told her that Thatcher had hired him one of the pack to help him.

The door opened and closed, and she looked over at Thatcher when he joined them. Rogen noticed right away that his hair was wet. Turning away, she had to wipe tears from her eyes. He'd done this for her brother, without wanting anything in return.

"Did you see his latest project?" She nodded but didn't look. "Come here, Rogen. Just let me hold you for a moment or two."

She went to him, laying her head on his chest. After she told him she was sorry, he lifted her head up by a finger to her chin. He smiled. It was sexy, and yet still little boy charming.

"Thank you. For this and for my office. It's really nice in here." He laughed and told her that he had an ulterior motive for doing this for Jamie. "You want something from him?"

Rogen stiffened and started to pull away when he pulled her tightly against him again. "Cool your overactive mind. I don't want anything other than a piece or two of his work. I was showing you this one because it's my parents' home. Before they moved to where they are now. It had been in their family for decades before my mom hit the lottery when we were still in high school. And he's doing it from photographs for them."

She looked at it then. The picture was blurred a little, black and white with a curl of smoke coming out of the top. It was stuck to a clipboard, just as her brother always did his work, and there were notes all around it. The color of the shutters, the wood that had been used, as well as the kind of trees; all of them, unrecognizable in the photograph, were apple trees.

The work that Jamie had finished so far was amazing. He had the strips of wood in the form of the house nearly finished. The curl of smoke was just the right color of grays and white. There were trees too, without the fruit just yet, and there were a couple of clouds in the sky that made her think there was impending rain.

Once Jamie had the entire thing cut out the way he wanted it, he would then fit it together perfectly before putting the wood in the correct order in the frame. Rogen ran her fingers over the front door to the little home. It was as smooth as she had expected it to be.

"I don't think he's ever done anything with a photo before. Usually he does things that he thinks up." Thatcher told her that Jamie had been very excited about getting a start on it. "It's beautiful. You lived here? All eight of you?"

"Yes. It was tight, but we were family, so it didn't matter that we were nearly on top of each other. I know that Mom was glad for the large yard to toss us out into when things got bad for her. But she loved us and made the house a nice home. I don't miss the smallness of the house, but there are times when I wish I had the same homey feeling that was there. This house, it's large and somewhat cold to me at times." She looked up at him. "I hope with you and Jamie here, it'll be what we need. A home. Shelter, as well as family."

"I don't know that much about making a house a home. I just put things in the places we've stayed that made me feel good." He said that he'd made sure that all of her things were brought here. "Thank you for that. Jamie, he can be picky about how his things are put in a box."

"I noticed that too. When my dad was trying to help

him pack up his clothes, he had to stop when Jamie had a meltdown." She looked over at her brother, who was working on some wood. "He's not violent, but he is loud, isn't he?"

"But he can be. Violent, I mean. He doesn't know his own strength sometimes, and he will hit rather than let you touch him." Thatcher nodded as he watched her brother. "He thinks a great deal of you, Thatcher."

"How do you feel about me? You don't have to tell me what you think I want to hear. I mean, your undying love would be nice, but I can handle it if you only like me a little." She laughed, telling him that she liked him a little. "Then I have something to work on. Oh, before I forget, Winnie gave me a cell phone. She said that there was one in your office for you in the safe. Took me a few to figure out that she'd had one put in. She's sort of scary smart too, isn't she?"

"Yes. As I mentioned before, I trained her for the job she has now. Winnie is smart and can do anything you wish her to do. If you need anything, including something for me, you're to call her direct. Donaldson, as we've talked about before, is a moron, but he's easy to fob off most of the time."

"You don't trust him." She said that she rarely trusted anyone. "Me? Do you trust me? Again, I would rather you told me the truth than something I want to hear."

"Yes. I don't know why, but I trust you. And your brothers, the ones that I met. Your mom, she's wonderful. Your dad is too, but he's a little...I guess you could call it out there. Where does he come up with those outlandish sayings?" Thatcher said that he made most of them up. "Yes, I can see that. But I trust him too. I don't know why, so don't ask me, but I trust your family. If not, I'd have you killed."

She walked away from him then, to see what Jamie was doing. Rogen knew he was trying to figure out if she was joking or not. She wasn't, but it would be good for him to think that she was for a little while. Rogen wouldn't hesitate for a moment to have him dead if he ever did anything to hurt her or Jamie.

~*~

"What does this mean?" Lisha Hall hadn't learned to read when she was younger and had thought it stupid to try and learn now. She could pick out a few words and know them. Her first and last name mostly, and little words that did you no good if you didn't know what the rest of them meant. "It has our name on it. See? Hall."

"It says.... Let me focus it a minute here." While she couldn't read, Jimmy couldn't see well close up. Distances weren't that bad, but close up stuff hurt his head, he told her. No one even made glasses that would make the words big enough for him, Lisha thought. "I don't rightly know. Something about Rogen. I have to take it to the window for better light."

"At least I can admit I can't read. You won't admit that you can't see your hand in front of your face." Jimmy told her that she'd be able to read his mind when he stuck his fist in her head. "Is that even a good threat? Christ, Jimmy. You'll have to do better than that if you're going to shit talk to me."

They never hit each other. They rarely argued past just saying things. They'd had a lot of ups and downs throughout their marriage, and some of them were really down. Just the other day, Jimmy had found out that he had sarcoma—stage four soft tissue cancer. They didn't give him long to live, as it was inoperable. He had even less time for him to be considered active.

"It doesn't even say where this is from. For all we know it could be from right across the street." She looked out the window and shivered. The only thing across the street from them was a trash dump. Lisha hoped that her kid would do better than that. "I'm going to call the newspaper office and ask them what they know. Surely, they would know where this came from if they printed it, don't you think?"

She did but doubted that Jimmy would get any answers. All those HIPPO rules, or whatever they were called, was fucking up a lot of things nowadays. As she laid back on the bed, in the only room that was at least a little cleaned up, she thought about Rogen. The girl had been smart, she'd give her that.

"Too smart for her own good, if you ask me." The kid was forever getting into their business. Why, she'd even had the nerve to balance their checkbook when Lisha told her that she didn't know if they had any money or not. Turned out that not only didn't they have any money, but they were in the hole about two hundred dollars. Bounced check fees were a killer.

But it was her knowing how to save her brother that had shocked them all. And to find out that not only could she read well, but she could run a computer too. Rogen had been close to her forth birthday when she'd saved his life and called the ambulance, all the while her and Jimmy had been standing there with their mouths open. They'd been lucky no one had believed her when Rogen had told them that they'd tried to kill him.

After that, not only did they watch what they said around her, but they also were careful about what they did to Jamie. Rogen seemed to be around every corner waiting on them. She'd even taken to letting her brother sleep in her room on the floor, like he was nothing but a puppy.

Lisha had hated Jamie since the day she'd found out that

he'd ruined her for other children. He'd been so big, and—well, she'd not really taken good care of herself, so when he was born, he tore her up inside. Not only that, but he'd made it so she'd not be able to carry another child even if she was to get pregnant again.

"Fucking dip shit." For months, even years before Rogen had become his watcher, Lisha had tried everything to get Jamie out of her life. To make him suffer as his daddy and she had. Her and Jimmy had wanted ten children, enough so that they'd be able to live in the lap of luxury for the rest of their lives on the government's dime.

But that had never happened. And when they'd gone to the welfare office to tell them that they had a dummy in the house, a note had been on their file that said that they were not only to be turned down for any extra income, but they were to be cut off from all government help. Lisha had always blamed that on Rogen. Jimmy didn't think it was possible for her to have done anything like that, not being so young, but Lisha had known better.

"I just got off the phone with the newspaper. They are rude, did you know that? Anyway, they won't tell me where the article originated from, only what it said." She asked him if she'd read it to him. "Sort of. They told me that Rogen Hall was considered a hero for saving a family from a burning car. Something about it being a great risk to herself, but I don't get that. Why would she even bother if they weren't her family? I guess I will never understand her. Rogen will always be a mystery to me."

"To both of us. When was the last time you heard from her? It had to be a while ago." He told her. "Six years? Wow, never would have thought that. Christ, really? Six years? I wonder if I'd even know what she looked like now."

"She'd never be as beautiful as you are, my love." She loved him for that, and he tossed the paper on the bed. "I'm going to go and see if I can rustle us up something to eat. You suppose a good faerie came in and cleaned up the kitchen? I'm getting sorely sick of living like this. It's much too late to try and clean it up now, don't you think?"

"Yes. We should have done it years ago, I guess."

They were hoarders. And worse than that, they never cleaned up after themselves—really, never. When they cooked, the pans were put in the sink to "soak." They only used paper plates and plastic forks. Those were tossed away. And the only reason a pan or something would get washed was because they needed to use it again. The only thing that ever got cleaned up was the coffee maker, and that had better be clean at all times, she thought.

Making her way through the piles of newspapers, she nearly fell over a stack of books. Neither of them read, and why they had kept them was beyond her. But they kept everything. Even if it broke down, fell apart, or even caught fire, as a few of the fans they'd gotten had, they would just toss it aside and go out and find another one. Thank God for auctions.

Their entire house had been furnished at some time in auctions. They'd sell off the good stuff if they didn't want it, then keep the rest until they needed cash for something. Or it simply ended up in a corner with the rest of the crap. Lisha was just bypassing a stack of empty cans when she heard someone at the front door.

Answering it, she made sure not to allow whoever it was to be able to see inside. They'd been living there since before the kids had been born, and so far as she could remember, no one had been at their door since the kids left. She asked the woman there what she might want.

"I saw in the paper that your kid is a hero. I wanted to come over and ask you what you might have thought of that. I'm sure you're not proud of her." Lisha, no longer concerned about what this woman saw, opened the door wider. "Also, I don't know if you are aware of this, since I have never seen you go to the mail box, but they've bought up the houses along this block, and you have to move out. I would have told you when the letter first came out, but...well, I don't like you, so I'm telling you today because this is the last day you have to get out. They start bulldozing them in the morning."

The woman, Lisha had no idea what her name was, left her standing there, cackling as she left—actually cackling as she walked away. Closing the door, Lisha looked at the paper in her hands. It was bright blue and the lettering was huge at the top. But she could see the numbers on it. Thirty and then a twenty-two. Running to the kitchen, she found Jimmy looking at the instructions on a label.

"We have to move." Jimmy stared at her with that blank look. "Here, look at this. It's a notice of some kind. Jimmy, they're going to tear down our house. A woman just came over and told me that today is our last day we can live here."

"I wondered why no one was harping on us about rent being due again. It's been a few months." He took the paper to the window, and she had to wonder again why he did that. Was there some sort of magic that came in that helped him see it better? "You're right. We have to be out of here by six tonight."

They both looked at the clock, and Jimmy wondered aloud if it was working or not. Pulling out her phone, she knew that there wasn't any minutes left on it, but it kept the right time. It was five minutes until six now.

"What are we going to do now?" Jimmy said he didn't know. "We don't have any money to move. And what will happen to all our things? We've worked hard on saving things for a rainy day."

They'd only started hoarding when the trash wasn't picked up. After that, it was sort of fun seeing how high they could stack shit, and which one of them would be the one to topple it all. Just the other day it had taken Jimmy an hour to dig her out of the newspaper stack that had fallen over onto her. They'd both been laughing so hard, she thought she was going to be there forever.

"I guess we just take what we need." She looked around when he did. "I don't have any idea what that would be either, love. Perhaps we can get some of our cleanest clothes? Some of the things that we can sell. I don't know where we're going to put ourselves after this, but we can't live here anymore. That bastard of a landlord, he should have told us what was going on. Not let us be in the dark."

"She told me that notices went out and we didn't check our mail." Jimmy said that was possible. "Yes, so I guess we got nothing out of this. Damn it all to hell and back, Jimmy. This is our home."

"It was, love, it was. But now we have to move on." He was being terribly calm about all this. She asked him what was going on. "Look at the newspaper that came a few days ago. I never had time to put it on the stack after you knocked that other one over."

Lisha looked at it but didn't see anything about it. It said their last name and that was about all she could tell. He told her to look at the license plate on the car.

"It's all blurry, Jimmy. What are you trying to tell me?" He picked it up and showed her what an Ohio license plate looked like with the one on the map on the wall. "They're the same. I mean, all but the numbers that you can't see, it's Ohio."

"Yes. Wherever Rogen is, she's been in Ohio. I don't know if she lives there or is just going through. But she's been to Ohio, and we're going to go there and find her." Lisha asked him why they'd do a fool thing like that. "Because, my dear wife, she might have a few bucks for us to take from her. And if she don't, then we'll sell her off to someone. It's the least she can do for her old parents, don't you think?"

"Yes, she can do that. But how do we get to her? That has to be a long way away, don't you think?" He said it would take several days to get there, no matter what they drove. "Okay, so how do you propose we get to her, and also eat and sleep?"

Jimmy said he was working on it, and he'd have it in a bit. For her to start gathering up some things they could sell off, but to make it little. When he left her, she looked out the window to see that everyone on the street had waited until the last minute, it appeared. There were all kinds of cars and trucks loading up at every house. Lisha didn't have any idea how they were going to keep their things after leaving, but she was going to pack up as much as they could.

Chapter 5

The last of the computers was set up, and Thatcher looked at the row after row of monitors. He had no idea how she was going to keep track of all of them, but then, he could barely keep track of one, much less twelve of them. Going to where she was standing, stretching her back, he rubbed her shoulders and asked her if she was finished.

"As much as I can be until they get me the cables that I need." He nodded and kissed her on the neck. "What do you have in mind?"

Thatcher's mind went into overdrive with all the things that had been on his mind all night. It was nearly midnight now, and while exhausted, he wanted her still. But he let out a breath and knew that he could wait for her.

"I was thinking that you could go and change into a cat. There is a full moon out, and you should be able to play without being seen." She tensed up. "Or not. It's up to you. But as your doctor, I'd say you are more than ready to do this, Rogen. And you need to get used to her so that if you do have to shift or need to, then you know what to do to walk and to move."

"I've been looking it up on your computer. It'll be harder, I think, than just walking like I am now." He said she'd be walking on four feet instead of just the two. "I'm also to understand that I'd be able to be sneaky too. I think I'd like that."

"Sneaky, is it? Who do you have to be sneaky to?" She told him about his brother Houston hiding behind corners and jumping out at her. "Yes, he loves to do that to me as well. Or anyone else that he can catch off guard. But never our parents. Mom would brain him, and Dad would knock him out. If he lived that long."

They were laughing as they made their way out into the yard. It was getting chilly out, and as soon as she set the lock, a computerized one, he told her what to do when she was ready.

"Just close your eyes and think of her. You might want to be naked, however. When you shift with clothes on, you shred them. The cat will be much larger than you are." She looked at him. "I swear, Rogen. Watch me."

He let his cat take him and felt the tear of his clothing. Thatcher didn't care. They were at home and getting into the house was easier now that they had a basement entrance. As he stretched out in the grassy yard, he let his claws extend, his fur stand up. It was a wonderful feeling being able to be his other self and not be scaring someone.

"You're beautiful. I know that I've said this before. But you're much too pretty to be such a beast." He told her that he loved her. "Why?"

What do you mean, why? She said that she didn't know him that well, and he didn't her. *You're my heart, Rogen. All that I could have ever hoped for in a mate. Someone that I want to show everyday how much I love you. Every day I want to tell you that you're beautiful, because you are. And most importantly, I love you because you will someday, soon I hope, love me back.*

Instead of saying anything to him, Rogen let her cat take her. He couldn't move. Her beauty was incredible. She was beautiful as a human, but as a cat — his cat — she was the most beautiful being that he'd ever seen.

When she took off running, falling more than getting very far, he sat down and watched her. Once she got the hang of walking, she was bouncing like a cat, jumping up and down like she was playing with a ball of yarn.

Aren't you coming out to play? He said that he was enjoying the view. *But I want to run with you. Do you have any idea how much fun this is? How everything feels now? The things that I can see? Oh my God, Thatcher, I think I do love you.*

She was running through the trees when what she'd said hit him. She loved him. Rogen had said that she loved him. He chose to ignore the think part, and enjoyed the part where she had said it.

Taking off after her, he was nearly to her when he saw that she had stopped running. Rogen was poised, her right front paw stopped in mid motion, her ears up and her tail still as death. He didn't move either except to look in the direction that she was. That was when he saw the big bear. And he wasn't a shifter.

Don't move. Rogen said that she wasn't. *He's not a shifter. I don't know where he came from, but he could be dangerous.*

The big bear roared but didn't move. He had to be able to see them both. If nothing else, he could smell them. Thatcher called for his family, all of them. This was more than he thought he could handle by himself.

There is a brown bear, not a shifter, in our woods behind the house. Rogen and I are here, and he's just staring at us. They all, almost in unison, said they were on their way. Then the bear dropped and charged at Rogen. *Shit, too late.*

The bear ran right at her and she still hadn't moved. Thatcher wasn't sure if she was frozen in fear or if she knew something that he didn't. Before he could get to her, the bear simply dropped. Even from where he stood, Thatcher knew that he was dead.

Thatcher didn't know where to look to see what had happened to the bear. But when a man dressed all in black with a mask on appeared, Thatcher noticed that he had a rifle over his shoulder. He nearly shit himself when Rogen ran at the man, knocking him to the ground.

Tigers came out of everywhere while he made his way cautiously to Rogen. She had her mouth over the man's neck, as well as her claws digging deeply into the man's cheek. He noticed in an abstract way that his body armor was no match for a pissed off tiger. Thatcher's mom came to stand by the rest of them, near the man's head. Mom cleared her throat before speaking

"Young man, did you shoot that bear? Blink once for yes and twice for no." He blinked once, his eyes wide with terror. "Rogen wants to know, and I'd make sure to not move when you answer me, if you thought the bear was going to attack her before you moved into his sight. Rogen, honey, why don't you lessen your grip on his throat so he can speak to me for you."

The man did nothing but keep his eyes wide, so mom asked him again if he thought the bear would have attacked if he'd not moved. Thatcher couldn't tell if Rogen had done what his mom asked, but apparently she had. The man answered.

"I thought he was coming for her." The low growl from

Rogen wasn't very encouraging. To any of them, Thatcher thought. "I might have made him attack. But I have never seen a black bear before and was worried— Holy mother fucking Christ, don't kill me."

"Young man, your language please." Thatcher laughed. Here was his mom, scolding a young soldier on his language when he had a large pissed off Bengal tiger at his neck. "She wants to know if you are aware of shifters."

"Yes, my wife is a wolf."

Mom nodded. "Did you know if that bear was a shifter or not? Were you completely sure that he was just a bear and not some little boy's father, a husband to someone out there that is going to wonder if her husband is coming home tonight? That's a wonderful thought, Rogen."

"I knew. I can tell what is what with paranormals." Rogen let him go, but the man didn't stand or even sit up. "I swear to you, Ms. Rogen, had that been a man, I would have only wounded him, not killed him. I swear on my own son's life, I wouldn't have killed him unless he harmed you."

Rogen looked at Thatcher and made her way slowly to the house. The soldier finally sat up but didn't stand. He looked at him, and Thatcher could see that he had no badge on and there was blood on his neck. Looking at his vest, he could see blood there too.

"I've upset her, haven't I? I'm sorry, Mr. Thatcher. I was told to keep her safe at all costs, and I did." Mom translated for Thatcher and told the young man that he'd done a good job. "You might think so, but she doesn't. And no offense to you, sir, but she's my boss."

Thatcher thought the men on their property worked for Winnie, or even Donaldson. He'd not realized that she had this sort of pull. After telling his mom to tell the man to clean up and get his wounds looked at, he went to the house. Shifting, Thatcher went in search of Rogen. She was at one of the many desks working, and he sat behind her and waited.

"I want you to do something for me. Will you teach the others what a shifter looks like as opposed to what a real animal is?" He said he'd do that and asked her if she was all right. "I don't know yet. I was willing to kill that man for shooting that bear, and I'm still pissed off that he did it. He was magnificent."

"He was more than likely sick. Bears, black bears, do not come around humans unless they are." She said that they were shifters. "We were, but we weren't the only people out there. Not counting the men that work for you, there are any number of us, as humans, that go out there and walk around. He could have smelled that at any time."

She turned to look at him, and he glanced at the screen she was working with. "I was so enthralled with him that I would have let him kill me. I have to go and talk to that man. I think I hurt him." Thatcher said not yet. "But I did hurt him."

"You did. But you also made him pay attention to what he was doing. Yes, he did what he had to do to keep you safe. But he also knew, which was your point. You wanted him to be aware he might have killed a person with a family. But family or not, if he had touched you, what the bear got would have been nothing compared to what I would have done to him." She nodded and looked at the monitor. "What is it you're tracking?"

"My parents. They are being evicted from their home soon, if not already. And no, before you ask, I didn't have anything to do with it." She turned off the monitor. "I want you to learn how to run this down here. Perhaps not as well as I can, but you need to know how to look a person up, and also be able to zero in on them to see what they're doing."

"Why would I need to do that? I'm not saying I don't want to learn—I'd very much like to see what it is you do. But why do you think I'd need to find someone?" She told him. "You want me to be able to find your parents and see if they're on their way. Where will you be when I'm doing this?"

"Working with Jamie. Grocery store. Out to lunch. Any number of things could keep me from finding them on my own. What if, say, I'm having lunch with your mom, who has invited me several times, by the way. But if we're having lunch and I see someone that looks like them, you can tell me if I'm full of shit or not." He told her he'd never tell her that. "You might think it, however. Thatcher, what happens to the bear now? I mean, we can't just leave it out there, can we?"

"No. But you'll be happy to know that the pack has taken it off the land, and they'll get rid of it. I'm not sure how, but there won't be a trace of it after they're done." She asked him if they would eat it. "Not if he was sick, no. But they might eat a great deal of him if he wasn't. Does that bother you?"

"It would have bothered me more if he'd just been wasted out there." She looked back at the monitors, then back at him. "I do love you, Thatcher. I love you very much."

"And I love you too, Rogen. And I would like to marry you. Soon." She asked him if he wanted her money. "Do you have any? Not that it matters. I have plenty enough for both of us and Jamie. Plus, any children we might have. Would you like children?"

"Oh yes, very much so." She went to him, sitting across his lap facing him. "Thatcher, will you take me to bed? Make love to me until the sun comes up? Or down again, I guess? I need you to make me yours."

"Gladly."

The sun was coming up when they were headed up the stairs. He carried her, not wanting her to wear herself out before he got the chance to. She nuzzled his neck, kissed his throat, and before they were in the bedroom, she had his skin so hot and his cock harder than he'd thought it had ever been.

~*~

Lisha was beginning to worry. It was nearly light out, and the bulldozers were all lined up at the end of their street. She had a feeling that they were going to start at nine right on the dot, but then she saw one of them back away. Maybe she was going to be able to keep her house.

The big silver camper came strolling in like it owned the place. The new truck had her wishing just once they'd had the money for something like that. But when it stopped in front of her house after turning around in the neighbor's yard, she stepped out on the porch to see who it was.

"Jimmy? Where did you get that thing?" He told her to get in and to shut up. Knowing that they were in trouble, she moved to get the suitcases, and he finally got out to help her. "I could only find one of the set of luggage we found a while back. And there really isn't much that we can sell off, I don't think."

"It doesn't matter. Just shut up and act like this is an everyday thing for us. Just leave it all behind. You'll understand when we get going." Always trusting Jimmy, she got into the big truck, needing his help to climb in, then they were let out again by the big dozer and were on their way. The truck was brand new. It even smelled new. "When we get down the road, we'll pull in someplace and I'll show you what we got. I tell you, Lisha, people are sure stupid with their things. I never had it so easy as I did getting this rig for us."

She turned in her seat to have a look at the monster. Lisha had never been camping a day in her life. Not if you didn't count the times they'd had to live out in the open when they'd not had the money to get home. Lisha asked him what they were supposed to do with this thing since neither of them knew the first thing about camping.

"Lisha, honey, you wait until you see the inside of this thing. It's a fucking mansion. And I did us right by it, too. I did steal it, yes, I'll tell you that. And the truck. But the truck was out on the lot running and there wasn't a soul around. I tell you, I drove it round for about two hours before I went back to the mall." She asked him if that was where he got it. "I got the plates at the mall. And I was pretty smart about it too. I took the plates off the back of one that looked like it could be this one's twin. And the camper, it had plates already. It was just sitting there in front of this big pretty house. I did the same thing with it. Found me one that looked just like it and swapped out the plates for it. Lisha, I couldn't have gotten us a better ride either."

When he finally pulled over, she was almost too excited to join him. Getting out of the truck had been easier, but she still bumped her knee badly. Lisha thought even if the place was a dump inside and nothing worked, she was so glad to see Jimmy excited and moving around that she would have stolen it herself.

Once he had the door opened up for her, stairs for her to get in just slid out like they were on some kind of machine. Jimmy told her that they were, and that was only the beginning. Once she was inside, Lisha just stared at it all. It was beautiful. So very beautiful.

"There are two bedrooms in this sucker. One in the back that you and me can use, and one in the front so if I'm feeling poorly I can move in there. The bathroom is bigger than ours was at home, and look at this, Lisha. I'm telling you, I hit the jackpot." He opened the door to a little place, and it was filled with food. "We can eat off this for some time, if we're careful."

There were luncheon meats and cheeses. Milk and eggs. Bacon and sausage, and those pop open biscuits. She touched the yogurts that were lined up, along with several bottles of water. When she opened the freezer part next to it, there was enough food in that to last them an entire month if they were careful with it.

She moved to the back of the camper, opening closets and other places as she passed. There was a bathroom with a shower in it, a toilet, as well as a pretty set of towels that were folded up and put in a cubby hole. Lisha felt like she was in a dream. All this, and it was theirs to use.

"I'm thinking that the people might have been leaving for someplace far away, and that's why it's ready to go like this. There are clothes in there too that you can wear. Not me; nothing that little for me." Yes, Lisha had forgotten how much weight he'd lost over the last few weeks. "And this will be fun for us. We can pull up in Ohio and find Rogen in style now."

"How did you know how to hook things up like this? I mean, it looks like you'd have to be pretty strong or something." She felt concerned that he'd taken it to the people and asked them how to hook up his stolen camper. Then he sat down at the little table like he was exhausted. "Jimmy, you didn't hurt yourself, did you?"

"No, but being this excited, it does take a lot out of me. Lisha, honey, you're bleeding." He got up again after making her have a seat. It was a bad cut, she saw, and might need some stitches. She asked him what to do. "Well, if it doesn't get any better in a couple of days, I'll take you to some kind of clinic and have them fix you up. But I think between the two of us, we can get you bandaged up. Don't you?"

"I do. Thank you." While he worked on her wound, they talked about the things that he'd discovered in the big rig, he called it. "We might be able to do this, honey. Don't you think?"

"I do. And I'm going to find us a nice place to pull in, and we'll sleep good tonight. I've been up all night, so I think I could sleep for a week, but this will be good for us both. When I get tired, I can just pull over, snooze in the back for a while, and move on. We'll make good time, you'll see." When he put the first aid kit back, he brought up something else he'd found. "It looks like one of those bank bags. Holy Moses, Lisha, what do you think is in it?"

It was huge and heavy, so she had to find herself a sharp knife to get it open. There was a lock on it, but she wasn't able to pick it. And while she was getting the knife, Jimmy worked on it and got it open. Lisha had been afraid that it was going to pop out some kind of blue shit, but all it did was spill money all over the table.

"There must be hundreds of dollars here."

Nodding to Jimmy, she asked him if he could write down numbers and she'd count them. She did know her numbers and counted out to ten wrapped stacks. Then she had Jimmy add up the numbers so they could tell. There were twenties and tens and a lot of hundreds in the bag. Also ones, but only about two wrappers of those.

"Okay, I'm going to tell you what we have and then I'll add them up." The numbers that she'd given him were written in huge lettering. Lisha carefully told him the count that she had for each kind of money. When he had them, he started multiplying the bill times the amount that they had.

She got up to check out the food in the big freezer.

There were steaks and roasts. Red meat was something that they didn't have a great deal of. There were frozen loaves of bread and rolls. Also some frozen fruit. The fridge was filled with things like the meats and cheeses that she'd seen before, but also salad fixings, small bottles of orange juice, and grape juice. When Jimmy cursed, she just knew that the money was all fake.

"There is almost a million dollars here, Lisha. Nine hundred and five thousand, four hundred. We're rich, baby. And I think this is from some kind of bank robbery or something. So you know what that means? Nobody is going to report it missing. Who in their right mind would do that? Call the police on money that they stole to report it stolen? No one. We'll be all right now." She hugged him and he hugged her back. "But we have to keep moving. And stay in cheap camping places. Get gas not on the highway, but in a town."

They decided to rest there for the day. And after eating a nice breakfast of eggs and bacon with toast, she cleaned up the kitchen and even did the dishes. This was new, it was theirs, and she wasn't going to have it looking like their home had. Not this place.

Lying down in the other bed, Lisha thought about the things that she was going to say to her daughter. But then she realized that with this money, they'd not have to go and see her. Lisha was all for that. She didn't much care for Rogen and was certain that she didn't like her any better. It wasn't really that, she supposed. Lisha was afraid that Rogen would spit in her face. And that would hurt. When he woke up, she'd talk to Jimmy about it and try and talk him into going someplace that was warm all the time.

Closing her eyes, she felt safe and comfortable. There were

things that she could do, she supposed, but right now all she wanted to do was rest and not worry. She thought of some of the things they should get, things that would make camping even better, but only thought about them. Jimmy made most of the decisions about money, and she wasn't going to change that now that they had a bit.

A house, her mind wandered over. A nice little house in a place that they'd not have to worry about the fucking neighbors. They'd had the worst living where they had been. Meddlesome and mean, they would call the police on them all the time about the trash in the yard. The way the lawn wasn't mowed. She didn't know how to do it, and Jimmy was ill. Why didn't they just do it themselves? Fuckers.

Letting sleep take her, she wondered briefly where Jamie was. Had Rogen finally tossed him to the side of the road? No, she'd not do that. She loved the little creep. She wondered if he was still alive. That would have been the way she'd have gotten rid of him, if Rogen hadn't stepped in. Christ, that kid was a pain in the ass. But Lisha would love for her to see her in this camper. Just to show off to her that her parents were not deadbeats, as she'd called them before leaving home.

Chapter 6

Thatcher watched her sleep. They'd made love until neither of them could move this morning, and he'd never felt so in love as he did right at this moment. When she opened her eyes and smiled at him, Thatcher revised his last thought. Now he was as happy as he'd ever been.

"You wore me out." He laughed and told her that he was thinking the same thing. "I don't suppose you'd like to wear me out again, would you? I don't want to force you—"

Thatcher picked her up and put her over his lap; his cock was in heaven and so was he. Her laughter made him laugh too. She was such a delight in anything they did together.

The way she was sitting on him, he thought he could live out the rest of his days like this. When she sat up slightly and guided him into her, Thatcher moaned. Christ, she was fucking perfect.

"Last night when you took me this way, all I could think about was your tiger and the way that he must take his mate." She rode him slowly, taking her time with her needs. "Then when you bit me on the shoulder, all I could think about was how hard I came, the way stars and tiny tigers danced around my head. Do you have any idea how wonderful it feels to have you so deep inside of me that I can almost swallow you?"

"Yes." He wanted to make her ride him faster, let him peak now instead of later. But the look on her face, the face of pure enjoyment, made him slow himself. Putting his need behind her own was difficult, but he thought in the end it would be well worth it.

Thatcher couldn't get enough of this woman. Not just sexually, though that was amazing, but just having her near him. Her laughter made him think life would go on forever. Her breath was like a fresh blooming flower in the spring and happiness, all rolled up into a neat loving package that was entirely his own.

When she said she was coming, screaming out her release, Thatcher watched her, marveling at the beauty that she was. And when she begged him for more, he rolled them to her back and pounded her hard, holding her hands above her head so that he could have his way with her.

"I need to touch you. Let me feel your skin." He told her no. Not yet. "Please, I want to come holding onto you until I can't any longer."

"You're much too greedy, did you know that? Just let me have my way with you, and then you can hold on. I think that you'll need to when I'm finished with you."

He suckled at her nipples, her breasts his to bite. Her body was his temple, his relief in life's stress. And when he felt his own release coming to him, he put it off just a little longer, letting her hands go so that he could bring her with him, both of them coming to peak at the same time.

"Come for me, love. Come and let me fill you with everything that I am." She screamed when he lifted her ass up to join his body tighter. "Again."

Rogen was coming the second time when he finally let go. Thatcher had never come so hard or for so long in his life. And when the second climax took him, he could only hold on long enough to bring Rogen again before he dropped on top of her, his body not just spent but dead to the world.

When he woke, he was alone in the bed and her side was cold, so he knew that she'd been up for a while. Getting out of bed was hard—his body was sore from all the love making and coming as he had. Taking a shower, he reached out to Rogen to find out if she was home or not. He found her in the basement and smiled. She was working hard on something.

Thatcher stopped by the kitchen to see if Rogen had eaten. "No. She said that she'd wait on you. But I don't think she thought it would be this long. I took her down some tea a bit ago. Whatever she's doing, it's very stressful for her, sir. She didn't even notice that I was there and gone, I don't think. You try and pull her away, and I'll make you up something to eat. Dinner is all right, isn't it?"

"Yes. And if I can't get her to get going—whatever she is doing, it must be important—I'll come up and get something for her to eat, all right?" Mrs. B said that was fine with her. "Good. Thank you for taking care of her."

"She's a right pleasure, she is. Nicest woman I've ever had the pleasure of working with." He kissed her on the cheek. "Don't you be doing things like that, now. You might make her a bit jealous of us."

Mrs. B was still laughing when he went to see Rogen. She had every light on in the place, and he noticed that there wasn't anything on the walls. They were as stark as a basement usually was. Also, and for some reason this bothered him more than anything, there were no plants down here. Surely if he had them set back from the electrical things, there could be a few, he thought.

"Did you know that there are over five thousand bank robberies a year? And that ninety-eight of them are solved?" She hadn't even looked in his direction before she started talking. "I can smell you. Is that weird?"

"No. Normal. Why are you looking for bank robberies?" She told him that was her job right now. Find the person that had robbed a bank in Colorado. "Do you know who it is?"

"Sort of. The persons who robbed the bank aren't the ones with the money." Thatcher sat down in one of the other half dozen office chairs. She looked at him. "I'm not sure what I'm looking at here, but it's very strange."

"Do you need me to look with you? I can be a fresh set of eyes. Oh, and dinner is about ready. Do you think we can go up and eat? I don't know about you, but I'm starving." She grinned and showed him the wrappers on her desk. "Good job. Would it be all right with you if I made the other half of this area into something more homey? Like add a few plants? A couple of rugs?"

"The men are coming back today to put a wall up in this part. I don't think it's very secure that you can see it from the door. So yes, that would be great. That way, we can enjoy ourselves down here and I won't have to look at anything. Maybe we can put out a deck or something, and a table so that we can have a little breakfast or something out there and in here."

"Excellent." She stood up and stretched. "How are you feeling this evening? I have to admit, I'm a little sore in places. I don't think I've ever been sore before."

"I'm sore too." They made their way to the other area in the basement. "Okay, let's get this started sometime soon.

Make it very homey for us. Jamie would love this too. By the way, he needs for you to come out and help him with one of the pieces of equipment. He said that you have to okay him on it before he can use it."

He was just getting his platter of food when the house phone rang. Mrs. B answered it and handed it to him. He was needed at the hospital and had to leave now. As much as he hated it, he knew that his job was important to someone today. After kissing Rogen and asking her to tell Jamie he'd get to him when he returned, he left. For as much as he loved his job and thought he was good at it, he really hated to leave home anymore.

There had been an accident on the highway, and there were two coming to his operating room. They were ready, waiting, when his nurse told him he had a phone call. Going to the phone that was covered in a nice plastic film, he said his name and asked who it was.

"It's Dawson. I figured that this was easier on your staff. Your patient died on the way in, but he's an organ donor. If you can do that for me, I might be able to save the oldest son. His heart has been damaged." He asked him if the paperwork was filled out. "It will be by the time he gets to you. I need this done now, Thatcher. The kids will have lost both their parents and the oldest child all in the same day. Please?"

"I'll do it. Just make sure they're typed and matched, Dawson, and we'll have it done when you're ready for me."

It would mean a longer day, but perhaps someone would be able to live after he was finished. Not only did he have to take the heart from the father, but he'd then have to transplant it into the son. It was hard work, often dangerous for the receiver, but the boy might live, and that was a better chance than he had right now.

The operating room wasn't set up for a transplant, so they had to work quickly in getting it ready. After making sure that everyone had eaten something and had gone to the bathroom, he was as ready as he'd ever be. All they had to do now was wait.

Dawson was going to assist him on the moves. He was a good doctor and a very good surgeon, but Dawson preferred to work in the emergency room more than where Thatcher worked. He said that he got to be there firsthand for anything that came along in the ER, and he never had the same day twice in a row. That was good for him. But Thatcher liked to have the same sort of day. Let him do surgery of any kind, especially when it came to working with the heart, and he was as happy as a camper.

Three and a half hours into the surgery, he was contacted by Rogen. She said she was sorry but asked if it was all right with him if she met with Shane. The pack master wanted to talk to her.

Are you afraid of him? She said no, but she didn't know how it worked with them, leader to leader—Shane being pack leader and Thatcher being in charge of a destruction. Then she asked him why they called themselves that. *My dad did that. He thought that a pack of wild cats, what he said we were when growing up, was an apt name for the group. There were very few of us in the area then, shifter tigers, so the council made him the leader by default. When he retired, I took over with about a dozen of us. If you want to meet with Shane, you can. You don't need my permission to do that. He's a good man, a better pack leader than we've had in a while, so go for it.*

She said that made sense and that she would meet with Shane. Rogen told him she loved him and closed the connection. He told Dawson what she'd wanted. He laughed a little, and Thatcher asked him what was so funny about that.

"She saved some of the members of the pack, an entire family, right?" Thatcher nodded as he worked. "All right then, what do you do when someone is kind enough to save another tiger for you? Or if they're doing something wrong? You reward them with a nice little mark on their skin that makes it so they're a member of your team, so to speak."

Thatcher thought of nothing else but her being marked by the alpha. It didn't bother him, not really, but he did wonder what Rogen would think about it. He could almost hear her telling Shane off, telling him that she wanted no such reward, that anyone would have done it.

As soon as they were finished with the operation, he showered and dressed for home. Dawson said that he'd keep an eye on the young man, and promised he'd call if needed.

As much as he hated to leave a patient, he thought it might be well worth being there today. Whatever was going on at home, he'd bet anything that a war was either going on or about to start. Thatcher laughed a great deal on the way to his home.

~*~

Shane had to bite his tongue several times in dealing with the pretty woman. She was stubborn, he had to hand it to her. But he was a pack leader, and she had done him a great service. All she had to do was put out her hand, accept his gift, and that would be the end of it. Instead, she said that she wasn't going to take it no matter what. He had a feeling that the no matter what was what it was going to come to. Finally, Thatcher was home.

"Hello, darling."

Shane didn't have a mate. Well, he'd had one, but she passed a very long time ago. Now he was left alone with two grown daughters who now had families of their own. Shane had no one to go home to at night anymore. Watching the couple in front of him, Shane wanted to find himself someone to have at home when he got there. Thatcher looked at him with a twinkle in his eye, as if he knew what he'd been dealing with.

"She is stubborn." Rogen said she was also right there. "You will take this gift I have for you, and you'll enjoy it."

He sounded like he was insane and let out a long breath just as Thatcher sat down. Perhaps he could reason with him. His wife was certainly one to test a man's patience.

"Did you know that my mom said that you needed a housekeeper?" Shane asked Thatcher what the fuck he was talking about. "Your house. It's in disarray, and you haven't dusted, Mom told me, in months."

"I have no idea what you or your mother is talking about. What I want you to do, Thatcher, is make her take my gift. She's being very stubborn, and I don't have time for it." Rogen told him to go home then. "See what I mean? She's should be listening to me. I'm a pack leader, and I have a fucking gift for her."

"You know what? I've already had to make my cat take down one man, and you might just be her first kill." Rogen stood up, and so did Shane. When he looked at him, Thatcher couldn't help it, he laughed. Rogen continued. "You sit your ass right down on that couch, and you fucking will listen to me."

Shane sat. Then he looked at Thatcher, shocked. Yes, she'd just made him sit down. He was an alpha, for God's sake. But he'd be lucky if she didn't make him beg before long.

~*~

"Now. I saved those people not for you to come here and

make me feel like I've done you a disservice, but because *they* were nice to me." The indication that he wasn't being nice was very clear, Thatcher thought. "If you want to make me so that the next time I see an accident I have to weigh it against putting up with your bullshit, then that's fine, I guess. It'll be on your head if anyone dies from it."

"Now you see here—" She snapped her fingers and pointed to the couch, and Shane sat again. "How the fuck are you doing that?"

"Because, you fucking moron, you might be the leader of a bunch of dogs, but I'm a leader of a bunch of fucking cats. And if you were to slowly turn around and look in the yard, you'd see that each of my tigers is waiting for me to signal before they come in here and tear your ass up." Shane did look, then turned back to Rogen. "Are we finished seeing who has the longest stream of piss?"

"Yes. And my apologies. You're nothing like any woman I've ever worked with before." She said that she wasn't working with him. "Yes, that much I've come to realize. But I am sorry. I don't understand what's going on right now, but I am sorry."

"My mom said that you're out of touch with women." Shane told Thatcher that was the truth. "Yes, and the fact that you thought that I'd tell Rogen what to do, or even step in for her, shows me that you also have been missing out on talking to people in general. You can't order them around anymore, Shane. Women are much smarter than we give them credit for."

"I'm beginning to see that." Shane stood up, then went down on one knee. "I am profoundly sorry for treating you like a bimbo, as well as an idiot. The reason that I'm saying bimbo is because Beth—you saved her family—said that I was treating her like one when I tried...well, it's not important. I was an idiot all around today."

"Yes, but I won't hold that against you this time." Shane laughed. It sounded surprised, as if it had been a while since he'd done it. Thatcher felt sorry for the older man. "Did you know that you have squatters on your land?"

"No. We don't cover it all, but most of it. How did you find out?" She didn't answer him, and Shane's look at him didn't get him anything either. "Do I not want to know? Or is this a case of you having to kill me if you told me?"

"The latter. They're also stealing your power source, as well as hunting on your land. There are six men that I've counted, as well as a truck that comes in once a week to drop off more food and takes things away. I have the name of the delivery company." Shane asked her if she'd help him. "Yes. But when I do, it's best if you stay out of the way. I don't want anyone killed over this."

"Seriously, do I want to know how it is you know all this?"

Rogen told him that she really would have to kill him, because no paperwork had come back on him as yet. She'd tell him or have him killed, depending on what everything said.

"You're serious." Rogen told him she was. "I don't understand any of this, but I believe you. And even when my paperwork comes back to you clean, I don't know if I want to know then either. But I would like, if you can, for you to get the squatters off the land. I don't want you to kill them...will you have to?"

She didn't even blink at Shane, and Thatcher was sure that was what scared the older man. Thatcher could see that he was confused, but he didn't ask any more questions. When

Shane sat down again, he looked defeated.

"I'm losing my pack." Thatcher asked him why. "There is a bigger group coming to town in a few days, and he'll kill me and my daughters. Because, like your wife here, my daughters will try and tear into whoever he mates them with if he tries. They're meaner than I am and should be pack leaders. But I've not turned it over to either of them because of this threat."

"If you want, Rogen and I can help you with that. I don't want them to be hurt any more than I want you to be." Shane thanked him. "Shane, we can help you. Just tell us what you need."

"I don't know at this point. He knows that I have my girls, so there isn't any hiding them. He also knows that I'm not as young as I used to be. That alone will get me killed. He's going to come in, take over, and then he'll kill my entire pack just for the land that we have." Thatcher asked if he could just turn it over to him and not get hurt. "No. I mean, I could, yes, but he'd still kill them all. It's happened before with this alpha. He comes in, destroys the pack that was there, and lives on the land until either he is run off by the authorities or—and this is what scares me—he uses up the land and makes it so no one can make it a sustainable place to live."

"What's his name?" Rogen stood up when he gave her the name. "Give me two minutes. I have a message that says I have your paperwork. And that you pass. Come with us."

Shane looked at him after Rogen left. "She said it all came back enough so that she can trust you." Shane nodded and said that he was still a little afraid. "Yes, you should be with her. She's not what you'd call a normal working woman. What she does really will get you killed. And while she might not pull the trigger, you'll be just as dead."

"You are not helping, if you want the truth." Thatcher

stood up and brought his buddy with him. "Do I really want to know what she has going on? I mean, if something happens and I no longer pass whatever test she has on me, then will she hunt me down?"

"No, never that." Shane told him that was a relief. "You'll never know until you're dead. And I'm not joking. She is that badassed."

"I know. I'm beginning to think she should be alpha and let me work under her." That had some merit, but Thatcher didn't say anything. Instead, he went to the locked door, put in his code, and then opened the door. "Thatcher, are you taking me to my death?"

"No. Too many witnesses know you're here." He didn't laugh, and neither did Shane. Things were about to get serious here, and Shane might well be on the top of the list of ones to die if he told anyone what he was about to see. Christ, this was more fun than he'd had in a long time.

Rogen was sitting at her computer when they entered the area. There were six men there, all of them armed but putting up walls, as if it were an everyday thing to need to have a gun to do this sort of work. Shane sat on Rogen's right and he on her left. She was so engrossed on her computer that he doubted that she would speak to them.

"This is where they are on your property. If you can see the truck there, they're offloading things. And this is the first time that I noticed that it was guns." Shane asked what they might be doing with that many guns. "I don't know, but I'm betting I can find out by the time my men get there."

The infrared flashed over ten men creeping through the woods close to where the squatters were. As he and Shane watched, Rogen moved to another computer and typed away. Shane watched the men, moving the mouse back and forth between the men and what looked to him like a camper.

"It's the alpha that's threatening you. He's been using the place as an off load for guns that he's selling." Shane moved to where Rogen was. "He's wanted by the Feds, as well as a couple of other government agencies. It's the real reason that he moves. Not because he wants to get the resources, but to keep one step ahead of the people after him. He burns the ground, as you said, so that there are no traces of where he's been."

"Holy shit. Look at that load he has." Rogen put a headset on her head and spoke quietly into the mic. Shane asked her, just as quietly, how long before they picked him up. She didn't answer because she was busy, but Thatcher had a feeling that they weren't going to be heard from again. When the men she had out there stopped moving, Thatcher watched them closely.

Rogen turned to them both as she continued talking into the headset. Thatcher didn't want to see what was going to happen next, but it was sort of like a train wreck. He just couldn't look away. It was then that he realized that Rogen wasn't speaking English. While he didn't know what it was, he was sure that he would have to learn it as well.

"Go."

That was all the signal that the men in the field needed, apparently, before they moved as a single unit on the place. There were flares of light—gunshots, he'd bet—then nothing. A helicopter was seen moving into the general area a few seconds later.

Rogen watched the men as things were moved around. Another truck arrived, then left after being loaded. The chopper lifted off, then the men were all gone. Thatcher didn't wonder where they'd gone, but it was like they were there then gone from the computer.

"Shane, I'd make both my daughters the new alphas if I were you. Stay on to guide them; they'll need it." Shane tore his eyes from the computer to look at him. "With you there, they'll be fine. I know it."

Rogen agreed and told him what he'd get for his help in this. "The reward for his capture will be given to you, but in cash. There will be no paper trail that you had anything to do with this. Alfred Derrick will never bother you or anyone else again."

"What about his pack?" Rogen told him that they'd blend in with the one he had now, after they were questioned. "You'll keep out the ones that had anything to do with Derrick? Anyone that is still a part of whatever he was up to?"

"As I said, Derrick will never bother you nor your pack again. And that means any of his underlings, as I've been told he calls them." Shane nodded, then looked at Rogen again. "Yes, I'll take the gift now. Only if you take one from me. I know that you will need more money, Shane. The pack you will inherit will be four times what you have now. And you'll need funds to help them. As of the moment that you leave here, there will be a hundred thousand dollars in your pack account. Is that all right with you?"

Thatcher had a moment of worry that Shane was going to turn them down, not take their help nor the money. But he was a smart man, and he proved it by nodding as he spoke again.

"Yes." When Shane didn't say anything else, Rogen seemed to understand. "Yes, you're right on all of it. The girls, my daughters, the money, and how much the money will come in handy for the things that will have to be gotten for that many people. So, yes, I'll take the money. How many more? I mean, four times is a lot of people."

"You're going to have a very large pack if my estimations are correct, Shane. About three thousand more. That's why I would suggest that you do as Thatcher said. Make them both the alphas. They can work together, I'm assuming?"

"Yes, very well as a matter of fact. This money, who is it coming from?" She didn't answer, but she would when they were alone. "All right. But you'll take my gift to you, correct?"

"I will, only if Thatcher can have it as well." Shane said that would be no problem. "Then I'm ready anytime you are."

Shane looked at her for a long time, and then turned to him. Thatcher had no idea what he might be going to say, but he could see tears in his eyes. For that alone, Thatcher hugged the man tightly against his chest.

"She saved my life. And that of my family and pack." Thatcher told Shane that he'd do the same for them. "Yes, I will. I will now. Whatever you need, I'll find some way to get it to you. On this, I swear to you with my life. I am yours. Forever."

He bit them both quickly, saying words over them that Thatcher didn't understand, nor did he think he ever would. When the small paw, that of a wolf, appeared on both their wrists, Thatcher knew that for as long as they lived, the pack would be theirs to call on. And even though he didn't know it, Shane would only have to ask, and Thatcher's destruction would be his to call upon too.

Chapter 7

Jimmy really was enjoying himself. It was nice having a clean bed to get into at night. Food on the table that was healthy and hot. Even Lisha was having fun. And the camper looked spic and span every day and night. They even did their laundry, having a blast at the laundry mat.

Having the money to afford glasses had helped him a great deal. He could read signs before he was up on them. The instructions on how to use things properly so he didn't break them. And having a nice GPS in the truck had helped Lisha with the driving too. They'd only been on the wrong path twice that he knew of, but it wasn't so bad now. They were having a good time being campers.

But he was hurting now. His body couldn't take too much more of the abuse he was putting on it by driving a great deal of the time, and then having to hook up when they stopped to camp. He thought he was doing a good job of keeping it from Lisha, but several days ago, she'd offered to drive. Jimmy took her up on it, perhaps a little too quickly, and went to the camper to lie down for a while. That had been going on for a week now.

He knew it was against the law for him to be doing that — going to the camper and sleeping while it was in motion. So far he'd only fallen out of bed the one time, and that had been when they were parked. Jimmy had gotten up and forgot where he was. So, in addition to the nice nasty bump on his forehead, he had a sprained ankle as well.

Limping to the bathroom, he did his business, as he'd called it forever, and picked up the little cell phone they had gotten several days ago. Telling Lisha he was awake and ready to join her, she would pull over into a rest stop or something. He had learned to brace himself for her stops, but she was getting better at that as well.

When she joined him, he was making sandwiches and she poured the tea. They were both eating better, and he was glad for that. She told him where they were. He had to stop what he was doing to just look out the window. Like that would make a difference as to which state they were in, he thought.

"Really? We're in Ohio already. I was thinking it would take us a bit longer." She said that she'd read the welcome sign four times before she believed it. "I'm so glad. And I've been thinking about what you said about seeing Rogen. I just want to say I'm sorry to her and Jamie. You can understand that, can't you, love? And when we talked about our kids, you seemed to think you'd like to do the same thing. I think we owe them that much, don't you? Plus, I'm so very excited to be living in a warmer state all the time, aren't you?"

"I am. And while I know that there will be more bugs all the time, the sunshine will be perfect. And living in this thing will let us pick up and go when we want to as well." She smoothed her hand over the table top. "I can't believe that no one has questioned us about this. I mean, we've been very careful about the money and all. But you'd think that someone somewhere would notice their truck being gone too."

Jimmy had thought of that as well. They were getting off pretty easily considering that not only had they stolen the camper and the truck, but someone's bank money too. He'd been meaning to check over the truck, just to see if it had anything in it that would give them a clue, but he'd not been up to it until today.

After lunch it was his turn to drive. But since they were in Ohio, they were willing to go a little slower, and Lisha sat with him while he drove. She did go over the glove box and anything else that she could reach. But there was nothing hidden in it that they could find, so he decided it wasn't worth getting worked up over.

They had a plan. They were going to stop in little towns, zig zagging across the state asking about the accident. Then when someone knew the family, they had a good idea that perhaps Rogen was nearby.

They'd talked over seeing Rogen. If Jamie was there, then that was all right with them too. They felt as if they'd been given a second chance with their lives. And if Rogen or Jamie wanted to be a part of that, they were great with that. If not...well, they'd not talked all that much about that part of it. They'd fucked up, they both knew it. And while making amends at this stage wasn't out of the question for them, it may well be for their children. Jimmy knew that they'd done them both wrong, and they had no one to blame but themselves.

The first place they stopped at didn't know the family. They were fine with that, but decided that they'd eat in the camper from now on. The food was too greasy and too fatty for them to enjoy. Being on a clean like diet had changed a great deal about them, Jimmy was happy to say. And he was having a good time being that way.

By dinner time they were both worn out, him especially. It was getting harder and harder for him to get out of bed every day and to do much more than moan and groan. Jimmy had given up trying to hide it from Lisha. Actually, it was getting difficult not to complain to everyone how badly he hurt. He had one thought, and one thought only — make it to tell Rogen and Jamie how sorry he was.

He'd not been a born again man. Jimmy thought himself too far gone for that. He'd not been a good parent, not even an okay one. Cruel and mean, that's what he'd been. And he, again, had no one to blame but himself for it. To tell his children that he loved them, that's what he wanted to do more than anything on this earth.

Making their way to the truck, Lisha said that she'd drive. He had it in his head that he wanted to lay down again, but he was fearful of that, really. What if he didn't wake up? What if — and this scared him more than anything else — he died while he was driving?

Jimmy was dying. He wasn't stupid enough to think that because they were now clean living and clean bodied that it would take away the cancer in his body. But he'd like to be able to live longer. Much too late for that, he told himself. Just live one day at a time and get to see Rogen and Jamie.

Every time they stopped, even just to stretch their legs or to get something fresh to drink, they'd ask about the kids. Jimmy had started crying at the last several stops because they didn't know anyone. Getting desperate now, Jimmy turned to Lisha.

"If I write a note for them, will you make sure they get it for me?" She shook her head. Tears were streaming down her face too. "Lisha, I'm not going to make it much further. We both know that. I'm dying. And I might make it, but in the event that I don't, I need for you to be sure and give them something for me."

"I don't want you to die, Jimmy. I need you. You're all I have in the world now." She wiped at the tears. "You write it to them, and I'll make sure they get it. But please, I'm begging you to please not die yet. I don't want to go on if you die."

"I know, love. I do. But I should have taken better care of myself. And of you. I have all these regrets that I can't make right. And now, I'm going to die without being able to ask my children, who I was the cruelest of all to, if they'll forgive me. Especially Jamie. We hurt him. More than just trying to kill him, we hurt his heart, and that pain hurts me more than anything. It haunts me, the look on Rogen's face that day. Every time I close my eyes, I see her face. I was a horrible parent."

"It wasn't just you, Jimmy. I was terrible too. We shouldn't have had kids if we wasn't going to take care of them right. And thinking that it was Jamie's fault that we didn't have more was just stupid. I know that now. None of it was his fault. He was just a baby wanting to come into the world, a world with us. They both deserved much better." She was sobbing and trying to keep them on the road. "I'm not going to be able to do this. I'm going to pull us over."

She did, and then sat there in the truck with him, both of them sobbing so hard that it was hard to catch their breath. They were horrible people, they told each other, and they were going to hell for it. But it wasn't anything like the hell they were both going through thinking back on how they'd treated the only people in the world that they should have truly loved.

They decided to rest at the next rest stop. Get out and see the trees, something that they'd been having fun identifying. Also, he needed to get out and move around. It was getting harder for him to simply get up after sitting for so long, and if he'd move around a bit more, then he could sit for longer periods of time.

After taking a nap, he felt better, and Jimmy sat in the truck again. He watched the trees and the homes. Some of them were like his own before the camper, piled high with junk and no one to clean up the yard. He regretted that too. Jimmy and Lisha had been terrible neighbors. There was just no end to how terrible they were to everyone. That night when he went to bed, for the first time in a while, Lisha slept with him. She'd not wanted to make him hurt if she rolled too close to him.

Breakfast was always a lite fair. They didn't want to be weighed down by food as they drove. He was in a better mood and felt a little better today. When they stopped for lunch, he made his way to the vending machines to pick up today's paper. And there on the front page was his daughter.

Not that he recognized her. No, she'd just been a mere child to him when she'd left them, but her name, along with the name of a doctor, was there for him to see. She apparently had married, and Jimmy had missed it.

His resolve to stop crying so much went down the tubes when he read the paper while standing in the little stand. There were names under the picture. She'd married into a large family. There was his son too, looking so grown up and handsome in his tux. And her husband's parents were there, looking like the nicest people in the world. Anyone, he figured, would be better than they had been.

Jimmy knew that he was feeling sorry for himself. He

hated that about himself lately, but he was in just too much pain to care what others thought of him right now. Making his way back to the camper, he showed the picture to Lisha, and pointed out the man that Rogen had married, as well as Jamie.

"He's a tall young man now, isn't he?" He sat down, the breakfast that they'd had, even lite as it was, weighing heavily in his belly. Lisha ran her fingers over the children. "I wouldn't have known either of them had it not been for you pointing them out to me."

"I had the same trouble. I did sort of recognize Rogen, but I would never have Jamie. The man she married, it says that he's a doctor. I'm happy for them both, aren't you?" She nodded and got up to clean up the mess that they'd made. "Lisha, what do you want to do about this? Go see them or not?"

"I don't know. Do you think it would be easy to get a phone number for them? Just to see if we'd be welcome? I don't think we will be, but you never know." He said that he could try the hospital where they were. "All right. I'll drive the rest of the way. I wouldn't imagine that it's all that far, would you?"

"No. I can look it up on my phone." He pulled out his phone and looked up the city that the newspaper said that they lived in. "Lisha, we're less than a hundred miles from them. I'll see if I can find a hospital near them."

It only took him ten minutes to find out that there was just one hospital close to where they lived. And it was a huge one too. He waited until they were driving before he called the number that he had for the main offices and waited on hold for only a moment before a cheery voice asked him if she could help him.

"Yes, I'm looking for a Doctor Thatcher Robinson. Could you please see if he'll call me back today, please?" She said if he held on one moment, she'd see if he was in the hospital. Before Jimmy could tell her that he just wanted him to call back, giving him enough time to get his heart rate lower, he was on hold again.

"Dr. Robinson, how may I help you?" He shuddered a little, and the man at the other end said his name again before talking. "Is this an emergency? Do you need an ambulance?"

"No. I'm all right. Right now anyway. Nervous, as you can imagine. Well, you might not be able to because—" He cleared his throat. "Yes, get on with it. I'm Jimmy Hall. You married my daughter recently."

"What is it you want, Mr. Hall? If you're thinking to disrupt their lives again, I'm telling you right now, you're going to regret it."

Jimmy started crying, babbling too. The man at the other end just waited until he was in more control of himself.

"I'd like to tell her and Jamie that I'm sorry."

~*~

Thatcher went to see his parents. He had something that he wanted to talk to them about, and he thought that of all the people that he needed help from, they were his best bet. His mom was the only one home, and she was working on a crossword puzzle when he joined her in the living room. She asked him what had happened.

"Nothing. Not yet anyway. I have a dilemma. I got a call from Jimmy Hall this morning. He wants to tell Rogen how sorry he is." His mom put the puzzle on the side table and looked worried. "I haven't told her yet, and I told Hall that I'd get back to him. That I needed to think if I wanted her to know. He seemed to understand, but he cried a great deal."

"Do you think that's what he really wants? To just tell her that he was sorry? I swear to you, son, if he hurts either of them, I'm going to take him out." Thatcher told his mom that he did believe him. "Then you let her decide. And Jamie. They're both stronger than anyone realizes, I think. But in this, I think that they need to be made aware of him and his wants, and that they need to make that decision. But you tell Rogen that we'll be there with them when and if they do."

"He's dying." Mom asked if that were true. "I'm not sure, but I believe him on that as well. He only has a few weeks, more than likely less than that if his symptoms are right that he told me about. Hall has stage four soft tissue sarcoma."

"Oh no. That poor man." Thatcher waited while his mom sat there. "Why did you come to me first, Thatcher? Surely you know that you have to tell Rogen and Jamie."

"I do. I don't want to, but I know that I have to. She's so happy, Mom. I don't want her to be depressed about this. Or be guilted into seeing him. I wanted you to tell me how to word this so that she's not thinking that I want her to see him." She asked if he did. "Yes. I don't know why, but it might be good for all of them if they spoke once more. He doesn't want to be a part of her life; he told me that several times. But he just wanted to tell her that he was a horrific parent and that he was sorry."

"That would be hard. On you as well as Rogen. Jamie, I don't think he'll be up for seeing them. He doesn't think that they should be alive. They tried to kill that young man and did in fact change the course of his life by what they did." Thatcher said that he knew that too. "Honey, in your heart, what do you want to say to her? You have to have some idea."

"I do, but wording it might be an issue with her. She's very bitter about them. And as I said, she's so happy right now." Mom told him to do it, tell her just like Jimmy had told him. "I thought that was what you'd say. I even took notes while I was talking to him. Just in case I needed to refer to them when I'm telling Rogen. I hope this goes as well as I'd like for it to, for her sake and Jamie's. I love that kid like one of my brothers."

"Your father and I were just discussing that this morning. I've adopted him in my heart, and so has he. He's not really that slow, is he? I mean, he does have a childlike way about him, but he's very smart. I'm betting that has to do solely with Rogen helping him." Thatcher said that she still worked with her every day. "Good for her. All right, son. You let me know what she says after you tell her. And you make sure she knows that I'm here for her, whenever she needs me. Poor darling. To have gone through so much and still come out on the high end of the stick. You did well with finding her, Thatcher. You couldn't have done better if I had picked her out for you myself."

Thatcher went home after telling his mom that they'd be over soon for dinner. Jamie had taken to eating out at restaurants with Thatcher's mom and dad almost nightly. It was good for all three of them. Jamie didn't let them sit on their butts at home, and Jamie got to have fun.

Rogen was working when he got there. She was buried deep into something, as well as and had a headset on. He didn't bother her with telling her he was home but watched her work. It was small wonder that she was trusted with this job. Rogen knew her shit, and she didn't take any shit from the men and women that worked for her.

"You do see that. It's right fucking in front of you. And as big as a barn. Again, it's an Oldsmobile, dark blue with four bald tires. You tell me again you can't see it and I'll come there and shove it up your ass." He could tell that wherever they were, there was a great deal of sand, and it was hot. "That's it. Give the soldier a prize. Plant the tracker on the back near the gas tank. He's still bitching about his bill."

He could almost hear the person at the other end but was not sure what they were saying. Rogen turned just enough to see him and winked. Thatcher blew her kisses. She wrote on a sheet of paper that she was going to be there for a little while longer, and did he want to take a run afterwards. Nodding that he would, she went back to work.

"He's coming out now. Make yourself one with the building." He could see the people on the monitors. She had about four of them going right now. One inside the restaurant, and two on the street level of the place. It took Thatcher a moment to realize that the fourth one was inside the Pontiac that they'd planted the tracker on. "The tracker is working. I have him now. Get your ass out of the car; he's coming. Once he leaves the area, you guys can go back to your unit. He must have slipped by me when I was looking around in the restaurant. Sorry guys."

She watched the car for several moments, but also the people as they walked away. One lingered, and she drew the camera closer to his face. It wasn't anyone that he knew, but she must have. Rogen told Private Jones to get his ass in gear.

The explosion took Thatcher's breath away. He'd not heard all of it, but enough to know that it was close. Rogen tossed her headset off and put her hands over her ears. She was cursing up a shit storm when he asked her if she was all right. It was then that he realized that the Private Jones was simply gone — there was nothing left of him but his rifle and one boot.

Before he could tell her to shut things down, she was

moving from the place she was at to the monitors that were down at the other end. She was moving the curser so quickly that all Thatcher saw was blurred blues and greens. When she had whatever she'd been looking for, the cameras stopped.

When Rogen called out for an air strike it surprised him. She not only directed them where to go by giving them the longitude and latitude, but she told them what the man was wearing and what he was doing.

"He'll be packed and out of there in about four seconds. If you don't get him there, I don't know if I can keep him under surveillance." He heard the man answer her at the other end. He told her that they were in sight of the location and were firing in one second. The building that the man had been in disappeared and the low flying jets zoomed by without another sound. "Job complete. Make sure you mark the area too. It's not a place they might use again, but we have to clean out the nest."

He had an idea what she meant but didn't ask. When she picked up the headset again and hung it on the hook by the computer, she turned to look at him. She looked pained, worried even, and he asked her to come sit on his lap.

"You need to be down here with me all the time, I think. When you hold me like this, it makes me feel better. I hate having to guide them to kill someone." He asked her if it had been necessary. "Yes. He killed an American soldier, and he'd continue doing so if he wasn't taken out. It's bad enough that the man that we're tracking needs to be taken out as well, but that isn't for me to say. They have an idea that he's got bigger bosses. How was your day?"

"I heard from your father today." Not the way that he wanted to tell her, but she didn't move except to stiffen up. "He wants to meet you and Jamie. I talked to him for a good hour, and he only wants to tell you both how sorry he is for being a shitty parent."

"What did you tell him?" Thatcher told her that it was up to her if she wanted to see him. "You're not going not make me? You're not going to say, 'It would do you good to finally end it with them'?"

"No. I won't tell you that. I think it would be good for you to be able to tell them off, but no, I'd never make you do anything." She got up off his lap and he felt chilled without her warmth. "He's dying. He has stage four soft tissue sarcoma. Cancer all over his major organs as well as his brain. He doesn't have long left."

"Why did he call you?" Thatcher told her what Jimmy had said, how he'd just wanted to leave a message, but they put it through. "Did he mention my mother?"

"Yes. He told me that he was teaching her to read while they drove. And that they're eating better, though he did mention it was too late for him, and they were getting out more. I even asked him how they got here. Jimmy told me that he wanted to talk to you about that as well. Both of us. Do you think Jamie will want to see them?" She said probably not, but she didn't know his mind. "Me either. I told him that I'd get back to him about it. That I wasn't going to talk you into anything, nor was I going to tell you to do it."

"You think I should? I'm not asking for you to tell me what to do, just a question." Thatcher told her that it couldn't do any harm for her to speak to them. "And if they get out of hand? Or want more from me than I'm willing to give?"

"My mother said that she'd take them out for you." Rogen laughed, and then asked him how she knew. "I went to her. For my own peace of mind. I didn't want you to do this unless you wanted to, so I asked her to show me how to tell you without coming across as demanding that you did it."

"Thank you for that." She paced a little bit more and then sat down. "I think they have bank robbery money. I've traced the money to a couple that robbed the bank and killed three people. Not my parents, but somehow they ended up with the truck that was used. Not somehow — they stole it. And so far as I can trace it, the people that did the deed have no idea who it is that took their truck. Because it was stolen, they can't involve the police either."

Thatcher laughed. It was funny, really. They robbed a bank, stole a truck to get away, only to end up with nothing. And a couple of people that probably needed it to see their children took it and had been living it up since. He told Rogen what he'd been thinking.

"No, they're not living it up. I don't think so anyway. The only money that has shown up from the robbery is two one hundred-dollar bills. One was used to buy food, the other for camping. I've found out that they're in a camper."

"You knew they were coming." She said that she'd hoped they weren't, but yes, she had an idea. "And I would assume that you've thought about what you'd say to them? If they showed up?"

"No. I mean, I did until you told me that he was dying and sorry. I don't know if I believe him on either thing, but I want to talk to Jamie first." Thatcher thought that was a good idea and told her. "Will you be there if I do want to see them?"

"I promise you, Rogen, I will never leave your side. This I promise to you." He hugged her and told her that he loved her. "Also, I wanted to warn you that the newspaper has a picture of us on our wedding day. I didn't think that they'd be able to print that without our permission."

"Free press. And it's fine. I got a copy of it, and I'm

thinking of having Jamie frame it." She smiled at him, and Thatcher felt his heart melt for her. "I'm going to keep my men on standby, just in case this goes badly."

He would never play poker with her. Right now, like a lot of the time, he had no idea if she was joking or not. Morgan said the same thing. She was just that good at keeping her face neutral.

Chapter 8

Lisha didn't want to get out of the truck. They'd not been able to park their camper anywhere, so she had it with her. Even Jimmy, who was sleeping more and more, wasn't aware that she'd made it all the way to Rogen's home. Sitting there, trying to decide what she should do, she finally got out just as someone came out of the big house.

They stared at each other for several minutes. It was Rogen; she knew who it was from the picture. Jimmy had cut it out of the paper and hung it on their refrigerator. It was silly, she supposed, but they had nothing else of their children. When Rogen came toward her, the big man came out too, but he never left the porch. Lisha was glad. If Rogen was going to cuss her out, she didn't need others to hear it.

"Hello, Mother." Lisha couldn't help it. She broke down. Sitting on her knees in the gravel, she cried hard. It had been so long since she'd heard those words that she thought never to hear again. "Where's Dad? Did he decide not to come?"

"No, he's resting. He's not well. We know that it's not right to be riding back there while we're driving, but he's been so ill." Lisha looked up at her daughter. "You're beautiful. I'm sure that your new husband tells you that a great deal."

"He does. And that he loves me. Something I never heard from you." It was no less than she deserved, and Lisha stood up. "Thatcher's family is here. They want to meet you."

"And you, Rogen, do you want to talk to me too? I know that we were never good people, and we've come to terms with that, I think. Coming to see you, we only wanted to tell you how sorry we were. You never did anything to us, but...I'm messing this all up." Rogen told her that she was doing fine. "We stole this truck and camper. I mean, we knew what we were doing, but we only had one thought, and that was to get to you and Jamie."

"He's not coming to see you. I'm not even sure that he wants to see either of you." Lisha nodded and looked away from the pain in Rogen's eyes. She had caused this, and there was no doubt in her mind that she was getting just what she deserved. "Why don't we get Dad, and then we can go in the house? That way we can talk."

"All right. He's usually out by now, when the camper stops. He must be nervous." She went to the back to the camper and tried the door. It was locked. "He's ever done that before. I guess he forgot. Your dad, he forgets a lot of the time. And he's in a great deal of pain. Let me just get the keys."

The keys were in the truck and she got them. Her hands were shaking so badly that she wasn't sure that she could open the door. When she finally got it open, still babbling to Rogen, Lisha went in first. She found Jimmy still sleeping. Lisha told Rogen that he was still in bed, that it wouldn't be a moment.

She saw the letter on the table that was addressed to

Rogen. There was also one for her on the microwave. That scared her more than anything. Jimmy had written to her as well. Hurrying to the bed where he was, she shook him several times before she realized that he was dead. Jimmy had died.

Screaming out her pain, because she was in so much of it, she called for Rogen. Her daughter was gone, and Lisha knew that she wasn't going to be with her right now. But her husband came in and asked her to move back. A doctor, Lisha remembered. Rogen was married to a doctor.

"I'm sorry, Mrs. Hall."

It was all she had to hear to know that her life partner, her best friend and lover, was really gone. In that second, Lisha blacked out. Jimmy was gone, and she didn't want to live any longer.

When she woke up, she was in a lovely bedroom with a quilt laying over her. There was someone in the room with her, an older woman that was working on the newspaper. Lisha asked her where she was.

"Rogen had you put in here to rest. Thatcher, my son, he's working on getting things squared away with Jimmy. Do you need anything? A drink of something?" She said that she didn't drink anymore. That it was one of the things that had hurt her family. "Yes, well, you have that about right. Would you like some water then?"

"No. My husband is gone." The woman said she knew that. "I don't know what I'm going to do now. He was all I had in the world."

"Really? Then why for pity's sake did you travel all the way across the United States to see the daughter and son you have?" She didn't care for the woman's tone and told her so. "I don't really care what you care about, Ms. Hall. You've done those children of yours a big disservice being like you were. They're good kids, and I love them like they're my own. Someone should have beaten you more as a child. Perhaps then you would have—"

"That's enough, Maggie." They both turned to the doorway where Rogen was standing. "Thank you for defending Jamie and me, but I'll take it from here. Would you please tell Mrs. B that we'll be one more for dinner?"

"Yes, of course." The woman kissed Rogen on the cheek and then hugged her. "Thatcher is going into town for a bit. When he gets back, we'll have dinner, all right?"

"Yes, thank you. For everything."

Before the door shut on the woman, Jamie made his way into the room with them. He didn't look happy, nor did he look like the child she'd hurt. Lisha asked him if he'd sit with her and Rogen.

"For Rogen, not you." Nodding, she watched as they sat side by side and held hands. They'd always been close, the two of them, and she envied that. "I have a good job. And my own money. But you're not getting any of it. Nothing from me."

"I didn't want anything from you. I promise. I only wanted to come and tell you how sorry I am for being such a shitty person and parent." Rogen said nothing, but Jamie glared at her. "I'm sorry. You don't have to believe me. In fact, I don't think I'd believe me either if I was in your shoes."

"Dad left you a letter, as well as one for me." She asked if she'd read it. "No, neither of them. One is addressed to you, and I'm not sure I want to know what he said to me as he was coming here."

"Again, I don't blame you. Your dad, he was so happy when we figured out where you lived. And scared. We didn't know if you'd want to see us or not." Rogen and Jamie both said that they didn't. "Yes. I guess, as I said, I'd not want to see me either. But we came here to tell you how sorry we were. That's not how it started out. We were going to come here and ask you for money. But we have some now."

"The bank robbery." Lisha asked her how she knew about that. "It's my job to know all about people that do shitty things. Why didn't you turn it in?"

"It was all we had after our home was taken from us. We stole the truck as well as the camper, yes. And found the money too. When we talked about it, coming to see you, each mile we covered together, we talked about how terrible we were. Your dad, he cried a great deal. He was so hurt." Rogen said they'd done nothing to them. "No, you're right, you didn't do anything, and you could have, I guess. No, he was crying because every day we'd think of something else that we'd done to the two of you. How we had treated you and what we'd done to Jamie. We were heartbroken at what kind of people we were. And we know that it was entirely our fault. We shouldn't have had children at all, not with the type of people we were. But we did have children, two of the best. Neither one of us realized it until it was too late. Because in every way possible, we hurt you and then shoved you out of our lives like you were no one to us."

Jamie left them then. Lisha didn't want him to, but she had no right to beg him to stay either. She looked at Rogen. Such a beautiful woman. Her heart was hardened, and she'd done that to her too. Looking around the room, she said it was a lovely home.

"It is. And if you think that I married Thatcher for it, then you'd be wrong. I love him with all my heart. And we plan on having children together. Ones that we'll love and hold dearly to us." Lisha nodded and bowed her head. Her own heart was shattering bit by bit.

When Rogen got up to pace, she didn't watch her. She had not only lost her husband today, but all her family. It was wrong to come here, she thought. No matter how they wanted to make amends, they should have gone on.

"I'm being especially cruel. I'm sorry." Lisha didn't know what to say, so didn't say anything. "You came here to unburden yourself, and I have no right to take that from you. I'm sorry."

"You have nothing to be sorry for, Rogen. I know now that we shouldn't have come here. We should have just.... Well, we should have done a lot of things and we didn't. And now that your father is gone...." Her heart hurt for losing him. "I don't even know why we bothered, honestly. Or what we expected."

"You expected something that I don't have to give you. Forgiveness. Perhaps I can give you that, but I'm sorry, there isn't any love in my heart for you. For either of you." Lisha thanked her. "I don't know you, nor do you know Jamie and myself. I'm not saying that you shouldn't have come here. You...I'm not sure what you should have done. I'm as confused and heartbroken as you are."

"Jimmy and I, we...we were terrible people. Not just as parents, though that was bad enough, but with people in general. And pigs. The clean camper has been such a joy to us—we never realized how nasty our house had become." Rogen looked out the window as Lisha sat up and on the side of the bed. "We didn't rob that bank that we found the money from. And I'll return the rest of it. We really didn't use all that much of it. Perhaps ten grand, your dad told me last night."

She thought about the conversation they'd had last

night — their last conversation, as it turned out. He'd told her that they'd give the money to the police and then tell them that they'd pay back what they'd spent. She had no idea what she was going to do now, without any money or Jimmy, but she'd do something.

"The money is yours." She asked Rogen what she'd said. "The camper too, along with the truck. I've taken care that no one will come looking for you about it, and you'll have a title to both as well. You can sell them if you wish or live in it. It belongs to you."

"How did you...? I don't want you to get into trouble over this." Rogen told her that she wouldn't. She had strings she could pull. "I don't know what to say. Thank you seems so — We've been looking over our shoulder since we left home. Thank you."

"Don't worry about it." Rogen turned to look at her. "This is not me telling you that things are fine with us. I don't know that they ever will be. But you can stay here. Like I said, you can live in the camper or not. But I have enough money to buy you a nice house and furnish it for you so that you can live close by. Not next door or with us, but close enough that if we have children, you can get to know them. I'm sorry, but I have to go. I have to do some work for another hour or so, then I'm free for the rest of the evening. If you want to talk then, I can do that."

"I...thank you." Rogen nodded and moved toward the door. "What about your dad? I don't even know...he's gone, Rogen. I don't know what to do now."

"The arrangements can be made tomorrow for Dad's funeral. No one is going to question anyone on why he died in the back of the camper. You will be fine." Lisha thanked her again. "I have to go. Missy, the upstairs maid, will help you out here. And show you around. I don't have a problem with you staying here for a while, but you can't live here. I...I'm not ready for that."

It was more than she deserved or had even hoped for. Getting up, she went to the bathroom and found a small basket of things like shampoo and other personal items. There were fluffy towels too. Taking a long shower sounded good, but she had nothing to wear. Coming out of the very lovely bathroom, a woman, Missy she thought, smiled at her.

"I have clothing for you, Mrs. Hall. Mrs. Robinson sent someone out right away for you to have things to wear while you're here. And there are a few things that you can use too, should you want." Lisha thanked her. "If you need anything after your shower, you have only to pick up the phone there by the bed and push six. I will be in the kitchen and will come up to show you around."

When she left her, Lisha looked at the clothing. She had expected it to be things like fancy dresses and high heels. But it was only sweaters and pants, comfy ones, and socks and under things. There were two black dresses in the closet that made Lisha remember that she'd have to bury her husband soon. Going to take a shower would wash away the tears. Lisha would make Jimmy proud of her, she thought.

~*~

Thatcher waited for the coroner to tell him the cause of death. He assisted as much as he could, but it was just as he'd been told by Jimmy. He'd died of complications of his body being riddled with cancer.

"I'd say that he'd been dead no more than a couple of hours when he was found. I'm sorry, Thatcher. I know he was your father-in-law. But I have to tell you, from the looks of things, I'm completely blown away that he lasted this long.

The man was in bad shape." Thatcher thanked him. "I can have the body ready for the funeral home in a few hours. I'm to understand that he wasn't from here. Do you know where you're going for the services?"

"My wife and mother-in-law are taking care of that tomorrow afternoon. She's pretty beat up, as you can imagine." Thatcher stood up and looked at the man he'd never met. "Billy, what would you do if this were your father-in-law? He wasn't a good man, not to my wife and her brother. He was heartless and a bastard. Both he and his wife. And they drove all the way across the United States, practically, to tell them that they were terrible and were sorry. I don't know how I feel, nor how I should feel about it."

He and Billy Wind had been friends since Thatcher had started med school. In fact, Billy was the one that had told him to switch his major from English lit to medicine. He'd even told him that he should be a surgeon when he was working one of classes with him. Friends didn't even cover what they'd become over the years.

"You say he came to make amends? Then I'd say that was a good thing in his corner. Sure, he died before he could. But I'm telling you right now, Thatcher, had my father done that, just made the trip? I'd be as happy as a clam with a fat pearl inside." Thatcher asked if he'd been abusive physically. "No, not him. He sexually abused both me and my brother. I found a way out of it and a way to get over it. I help others. But my brother, Tommy, he wasn't so lucky. Killed himself when he was only about ten. Poor kid. I never knew he was being done too. So twice a week, more if I can swing it, I go down to the shelter and talk to people. Mostly kids. And if I can't get them out—well, they do get out. But I won't go into that with you."

Thatcher thought about it as the man finished up with

Jimmy. "Billy, I'd like for you to see if they need a doctor down there. I don't have a great deal of time at the moment, but I can move things around over the next few weeks and spend a day or two there too. If you think they'd need me. I don't want to step on toes."

"They'd surely love to have you there, Thatcher. There are a few of them little fellas that need more than someone to talk to. They need someone to look after some of the abuse too." Thatcher said he'd set up a clinic there. "Good for you. I knew the first time you showed up at my class that you were going to be one of the good ones. Thanks, Thatcher. They'll surely love that."

Stopping by the emergency room to see his brother, he and Dawson decided that they'd have lunch today. It would be hospital food, but here it wasn't so bad. Not as bad as some that Thatcher had eaten in. As they waited in line to get their food paid for, he told his brother what he was going to be doing.

"I've actually been thinking about that place." He leaned in closely, talking just below a whisper. "I've had enough here, Thatcher. I swear to you, it gets harder and harder for me to come to work. So many children abused."

"I know what you mean." He did too. Thatcher couldn't count on both hands how many children he'd put back together in recent months. They sat in a part of the cafeteria where they'd not be overheard. "What do you plan to do? Leave here and put out a shingle of your own?"

"No. I've been really thinking about this hard for the last couple of months. I think I'd like to go back to school and be on the other end of the tests. Be a teacher. I think I can do it, don't you?" Thatcher said he'd told him to do that long ago. "Yes, well, I guess I had to figure it out on my own. This is a dead end. And so much is changing daily that it takes me almost my entire shift to get through the new policy changes in this place. I think that someone upstairs is just making some of this shit up as they go along. I got a memo yesterday that said that we had to wear our lab coats all the time, including our free time. Who the hell tells someone that? Don't I give enough blood, sweat, and tears here?"

"Here's a good one for you. I have a memo in my inbox that tells me that from now on I have to rinse out my gloves and try to reuse them. Or send them to another department to use. I'm keeping that one. I have a feeling that when it gets out, and it will, there will be hell to pay." Dawson pulled out his phone and told him that he had six more emails right now. "Anything I need to know about?"

"Yes, I'd say so. You're not going to like this one. Not one bit." Dawson handed him his phone just as Morgan joined them with a bag of fast food. He was munching down on a sub as big as his leg as he talked around his full mouth.

"I found out something that I think you both need to know." He looked around and Thatcher caught himself doing the same thing. When Morgan leaned in, he and Dawson did the same thing. "They're closing down this hospital. One of my students, their mother is on the board. The place is losing money every day. And they're sick of funding something this big that isn't making them much in the way of returns. I thought that saving lives would be the big thing, but apparently being a college professor of finance doesn't make me that smart."

"That could be the cause of all the cutbacks that I'm seeing in my department. I'm short on nurses daily because of someone taking them off the schedule. And no overtime, not even for doctors. Like we're supposed to just stop in the middle of stitching someone up and say, tough day for you. I'm off work." Dawson tossed his fork down. "Damn it, this isn't right. We need this place more than we need for them to make a huge profit."

Thatcher thought of Rogen and her ability to dig deeply into things and find information that few would have. He wanted to talk to her face to face, but he knew that the sooner he told his family that it was being looked into, the sooner they'd feel better.

Are you busy, love? She said that her and her mother were shopping for dresses. *You going to wear one?*

I don't know. Jamie told me that he's not wearing a suit but a nice shirt and pants. He said that he didn't know this man, didn't like him when he did, and he won't do it. I told him that was fine with me, so long as he behaved himself. You know what he did? He stuck his tongue out at me. I think that he's spending much too much time with your brother Jonas. He's a bad influence. But I love them both too much to complain. What did you need?

He told her what was going on with the hospital and that it might close up, and about the emails that he and Dawson had gotten. He asked her to hold on a moment. Dawson had something that he needed to read.

The email was addressed to everyone, and his name was in the subject line. When he read it the first time, Thatcher thought it was his brother playing a joke on him. After asking him about it and Dawson denying it, he told Rogen. She was fit to be tied, as he'd heard said by his mom.

So, you're leaving for greener pastures, are you? Were you planning on taking me with you, or are you just going to continue on with a bachelor life? Rogen laughed and said to give her a couple of hours here, then she'd have more information. *My mom is crying again. Not that I blame her, she feels all alone right now. But I have a feeling that it's more than that. I don't know. Could be that I don't want to think she's that grief stricken. I'll get back to you about the hospital thing later.*

He told the other two and asked them to please correct anyone that asked about this information. "I'm not leaving, that I know of. And if I do, I'd certainly not tell anyone through email. Christ, this is just shitty."

They finished their lunch and talked about different things about their jobs. Morgan had a degree in finance, but he'd never done much more than a few things with Jonas, who loved numbers. Teaching was all Morgan had ever wanted to do. And when the opening had come up a while back, he nearly jumped at the chance. Now he was working on tenure, as well as getting his PhD in his area of knowledge. Thatcher was very proud of his brothers, all five of them.

Morgan was a professor, and more than likely would be for the rest of his life. He was also one that got into trouble a great deal with women. Not that he harmed them, but they wanted him in ways that were not only against the rules but would cause Mom to kill him.

Houston was a potter. Few knew who he was other than the family and his agent, but his pieces, some larger than life and others small enough to fit into your palm, were world renowned. When he wasn't playing in the mud, as Dad called it, Houston helped teach handicapped children how to color and to paint. Thatcher thought that he enjoyed that more than he did anything else he did.

Beckett was...well, he did what he wanted when he wanted. Somedays he'd be working in a winery. Then he'd work the line at some factory. He was forever doing things that he both loved and hated. But it never stopped him from doing them. Someday Thatcher was going to pin him down and figure out why he did such a plethora of things. He more than likely didn't want to know the answer, but he'd ask anyway.

Jonas kept them all in money. He, like Morgan, loved numbers, but Jonas also liked to make a buck into a million. None of them, would never have to work again, the way that Jonas took care of them. And now he was helping Rogen with her money. Thatcher hadn't figured out how much Rogen had, but she did tell him that his name was on all her accounts. He didn't really care, Thatcher just loved the woman.

Dawson and he had become doctors. Both of them had finished up about the same time in college. Dawson was very smart and worked hard, but just lately, and he knew why now, he seemed to be unhappy at work. Thatcher hoped that Rogen could figure something out for them. This town needed a hospital close by.

Going home, he was ready to get into some work when he heard Rogen and Lisha come in. They were hot into an argument, and it sounded like it had been going on for a while. Thatcher knew better than to interrupt, so he waited for a lull in the loud conversation before he made himself known to them.

Chapter 9

Rogen tried very hard not to be upset with her mom. It was difficult when she was railroading her at every turn. First, she wanted to have Dad cremated, then not. She didn't like where he was going to be buried. Then the house that they looked at for her was much too big. There wasn't a garden at the next one. She didn't want to have to mow, if she didn't have to. Even after making sure that it was taken care of, she had a million and one things that were wrong with everything she showed her.

"Maybe I should just go back home." It was on the tip of Rogen's tongue to ask her where she was going to go when she got there but didn't. Not yet, at any rate. "Rogen, I just want to be able to be closer to you and Jamie. Why can't I just rent one of those assisted living places? They seem nice on the commercials."

"They might be, Lisha, but the problem is, you don't need assistance. I think we should focus on you living in a place where you can be active, yet not have to do a great deal." Rogen looked at him and begged him with her eyes to help.

When he smiled at her, she knew that he got it.

"Did you get a chance to get that information I need on the hospital, love?"

"No. I will though. Where did he hear that the hospital was shutting down?" Rogen would have jumped at any conversation for a break from her mom. "Why don't you take Mom to the next house on the list? And we picked out her dress for Dad's funeral. It's lovely, Thatcher. It looked really good on her."

Passing off her mother was mean, she knew that, but she didn't know what else to do. Her mother was being stubborn. Not that she wasn't as well, but Rogen didn't like dealing with small details when the larger ones were looming over her. Like her job. Something was off about it, and she needed to talk to Winnie.

Pulling up the hospital, it didn't take that much to crack into their accounts. What moron would use one-two-three-four as their passcode? Digging into their finances, she couldn't see a thing wrong until she found a file that was off limits because it had been encrypted. Putting in her program that would hopefully figure it out, she waited for it to run while sending a message to Winnie. Rogen got a message right back from her.

I can't meet you for lunch today, kiddo. I have a job that takes up all my time now. That was sort of odd. Winnie would meet her anytime. *Perhaps I can come over and see your new home? And pick up that picture from Jamie.*

She'd been to the house, several times. Telling her that her mom wanted to meet her as well, she waited for a response. When the phone rang, Rogen was sort of scared for her friend.

"I don't have long. Come get me." She said she would. "Today, now if you can. Bring Mom." Then the line went dead.

Bring Mom? As far as she knew, Winnie's mother had passed away. Did she mean her mom? Surely not. But she had to make a decision and make it now. Getting up from the computer, she let the program run and grabbed her keys. Whatever was going on, she needed to get to her right now.

Rogen opened the safe and pulled out her gun. Then she pulled out a second one just in case. Plenty of ammo was next. While she didn't know what was going on, being armed did make her feel slightly better. The knife in her sock pocket was there, so she reached out to Thatcher to let him know what was going on.

We're still here. Looking over some houses on the computer. She told him that she had to take her mom. *All right. But I'm going as well. I don't know what is going on, but you're not going alone.*

All right.

She ran up the stairs and Mom was ready to go. So was Thatcher. "I don't know what's going on, but here is a gun for you to use." When he didn't take it, she shoved it at him. "Look, as you said, we don't know what's going on, but I don't—"

"Oh, give it here." Her mom took the gun, checked the clip, and then racked one into the chamber. Rogen just stared at her. "What? I'm a grown woman, Rogen. I do know a few things that might surprise you."

Hurrying to the car, she told both Thatcher and Mom about Winnie. "She said to bring Mom. And since I know that her mom is gone, I guess it would mean you. Are you up for this, Mom? I don't want you to be hurt." Mom told her that was the nicest thing she'd said to her all day. "I'm sorry. I have too many pots on the stove, and some of them are boiling over. Please forgive me."

"Yes. I do. Always. Perhaps not in the past, but I do now." They were on the freeway in ten minutes. Her mom looked at her in the mirror, then looked away. "I don't know how to read. I'd like to learn. I'm terrified that you'll have children someday and they'll want me to read them a story. I don't know how."

Thatcher turned in his seat and looked at her mom. "There isn't any reason that you can't learn, Lisha. I know for a fact that my mom would help you. She used to be a teacher when we were younger. I can ask her for you if you want."

"I feel like such an embarrassment to you both. You have college educations, and I only went to fourth grade before my parents took me out to work at home. I didn't learn all that much, and I think now that they passed me to get me out of their room. My grandma lived with us—what a horrid woman she was. But I was responsible for her while my mom took care of the house." Rogen told her that she'd not known that. "No, we were very careful, your dad and I. And I would get so angry when you'd bring home your work and hang it on the refrigerator. I think that had a lot to do with how I treated you both. And then you started teaching Jamie, and I just...well, you know how I was. But I do want to learn to read. Please, Thatcher, would you please ask your mom? Tell her not to expect miracles, but if I could just read a little book once in a while, I'd be forever indebted to her."

Rogen drove for a few more miles before she pulled over, asking Thatcher to take over, she sat in the back with her mom. This was going to be hard—not on her mom, but herself—but she'd been so wrong. And so mean.

"I'm sorry." Mom patted her hands. "No, you don't understand. I was rushing you into things because I didn't want to be bothered with you. But now that I think on it, you did a good job of hiding it even today when we were out."

"Yes, I have an allergy to some materials. Wool mostly, but there is this one — I can't think of it right now — that breaks me out. Your dad, he wrote it down for me, but I don't know where that might be either." Rogen told her that they'd figure it out. "Also, Rogen, I want you to not include me in your family things. It's just not right that I've been away from you and you pretend that — "

"Don't. Don't do that. I was wrong, Mom. On so many levels. You have no idea...well, I guess you do. But I've been shoving you away since you got here. You should have told me, but that's not your fault either. I more than likely wouldn't have listened anyway." Rogen did something that she'd not done in decades, since she was a very small child. Rogen hugged her mom. Hugged her like she meant it.

They were both still teary when they made it to Columbus. The downtown office was nondescript; no one would ever know that it housed a large group of men and woman that kept the country safe. Messaging Winnie again, she told her that they were here and asked where to come in. Only a few minutes later, Winnie was coming out of the building.

"Hello, Mrs. Hall. My goodness, Rogen looks like you." She hugged Lisha and then Rogen. When she passed a thumb drive to her, Winnie then hugged Thatcher. "It's been a long time, Thatcher. How is your business going? Are you still on top of the world?"

Something occurred to Rogen as she stood there. Taking Winnie's hand into hers, she took it to her mouth and bit down on her finger. The connection was immediate and profound. She asked her friend not to freak out.

No, I won't. Oh, Rogen, I need to come with you. I can't stay here. She asked her if she was all right. But instead of answering her, she turned and looked around before pulling her sweater down and showed her the marks. *I don't know who did it, so don't ask. I was coming out of the printing room when someone grabbed me from behind.*

"Come on, we'll have some lunch." She looked at Thatcher when he spoke, and he shrugged. "I'm hungry. Come on, ladies. A man with three beautiful women at his side…well, it's the story of romance."

Rogen asked him what was going on, and all he needed to do was nod. She looked in that direction and saw someone at the window looking at them. Going across the street, they were all seated right away and ordered drinks first. Rogen wasn't even sure that she could eat a thing, she was so mad about her friend. It was her mom that spoke first.

"You know, I used to have this friend. He was an odd duck, but he'd follow me around like a puppy. I finally had to tell him that I was married, for the tenth time, and that I couldn't be his wife. It was like talking to a brick wall with him." She took a sip of her tea and smiled at Winnie. "Do you work with anyone like that? I mean, just someone that makes you feel like you need to slap him around a few times?"

Rogen was lost, but Winnie nodded. "Yes, I do. His name is Earl Fleming." Winnie looked at Rogen. "You know the name, don't you? He used to work with me at DC."

Winnie had never worked at DC that she knew of, but Rogen pulled out her tablet and began doing a search. Everything that she had that had Internet hookup was secure, and this was no different. After ordering her meal, she handed the device to Winnie.

"Those are pictures of our home. We have a lot of remodeling to do, but it's nice." The pictures on the tablet were not of her home, but of the men that were named Fleming that worked in the company. "There is one room that I particularly love, and that's the greenhouse room."

"This one is my favorite." She handed it back to her just as someone came in. Rogen knew him. It was one of the men that she'd had to deal with before. "You really should have me over, Rogen. It's been too long since we did girly things."

The man came to their table and stood behind Winnie. The panic in her eyes had Thatcher standing up. Whatever he was going to do or say was cut off when her mom stood up.

"I'm sorry, I must use the ladies' room." But when she went by Winnie's chair, she paused behind the man. "I'm not afraid to use this on you. You either drop the gun or I blow a hole in you that we'll be able to read a newspaper through. Drop it." Earl Fleming had just been taken down by her own mother.

Thatcher stood up then and took the gun from her mom. Mom went on to the bathroom while Winnie laid her head on the table and sobbed. Whatever was going on, Rogen was going to get to the bottom of it.

After calling in for some back up from her department, Donaldson came to the little deli. When Winnie went to him, hugging him to her, Rogen watched with shock. Donaldson and Winnie? Who knew?

"I had hopes that she'd call you. It's been hell trying to pretend to work while this madman was trying to kill her." Winnie bubbled out as to how Rogen's mom had saved her, and Rogen realized that Mom had been gone a while. Going to the bathroom, she found her on her knees throwing up.

"What was I thinking?" Rogen waited on her mom to come out of the stall. "I saw the gun and had a feeling that you had no idea what he was doing. So I just poked him in the back with the gun that I had and he did like I said."

Rogen hugged her mom for the second time that day. "Thank you for saving my dearest friend. And you're right, I had no idea. Are you all right?" Mom nodded and said she was fine now. "Good. And the next time I'm going on a mission, I'm going to take you with me. You're badassed, Mom."

They were both laughing when they came out of the bathroom. Fleming was gone, and Winnie was calmer now. Donaldson was buying them all lunch. It was the strangest afternoon she'd ever had.

~*~

"Yesterday when I was working at my desk, I got this strange feeling I was being watched. You know my routine, Rogen—I go to the gym then I come back to my office, change into my suit, and get to work. But I felt dirty. I was just getting ready to go back and shower again when I saw it. The little icon in the corner." Thatcher didn't know what that meant, but they had his full attention. "He had cloned my computer."

Now that, Thatcher knew what it meant. Rogen had several computers that she had cloned over the years, and could, with a couple of clicks, see a person as they worked. He'd been a little freaked out when he saw someone's nose hairs enlarged on one of her monitors, but after that, when he moved back, it was funny.

"Why didn't you call me yesterday?" Winnie handed Rogen her phone. Leaning over her shoulder, he watched as she played around with the phone before handing it back. "It's fixed now. Is that what all the cloak and dagger was about? And why on earth did you tell me to bring my mom? It worked out for the best, but how did you know that?"

"I didn't know. I only meant to warn you. I didn't even

know your mother was around. I was just trying to convey how much shit was going down." Winnie looked at Rogen's mom. "No offense, Mrs. Hall, but Rogen and I have been friends for a long time and have talked about our families. And if it makes you feel any better, mine are worse than you ever were."

Thatcher didn't think that was helping, but Lisha only patted her hand. "It's all right, dear. I'm turning a new leaf. And Rogen and Thatcher are going to help me. But I must say, if their days are like this, I might be happy to be a little off the beaten path. This was certainly nothing I ever encountered before." They all laughed, and it sounded like it was well meant. There was no force in it as he'd heard at home with Rogen and Lisha.

After Thatcher examined Winnie, they all went to the offices where Rogen reported. It was smaller than he'd thought it would be. But it was Winnie's office that he was impressed with. She was painfully organized and had sticky notes all around her computer. He asked her about the colorful notes.

"Rogen taught me this. Every day when you come to work, you make a job that you need to get done and stick it to the screen. There are different colors for different jobs." He asked about the blue ones. "Those are things that have to be done, but there is no deadline. The pink ones are for things I need to do for home. As you can see, there aren't that many of them. Not because my home is perfect, but because I just gave up in trying to get it done. The green ones are for things that can't wait and that I need to work on now."

"It's a nice sense of accomplishment when you get a note done. She'll remove it from the screen then tear it up. And she won't be able to add anything other than a green sticky until the next day. I loved leaving the office with only one or two notes to deal with." Rogen walked to him and he wrapped her into his arms as she continued. "You don't want to see my closet, however. It's a total mess of me just tossing shoes to the floor and never hanging things up that need to be. Thankfully, Mrs. B keeps me in clean clothing, as well as a nice neat closet."

After being shown around, they headed home. Lisha laid her head on the window and fell asleep, but Rogen was working on something with her small computer. Thatcher asked her a couple of questions, both of which he only got grunts to. Then he just gave up. Whatever she was working on, it was taking all her attention.

"Who are your board members? The ones that make the daily decisions?" After telling her the names, Thatcher asked her why. "The money is there—a great deal of it—but it's not being used for supplies or anything else that it's been earmarked for. In fact, I'd say that someone was intentionally not paying for things in order to have a nice fat account. But I don't know who it's for. Or what, for that matter."

"You're telling me that the money is there to pay the nurses that have been let go, as well as new doctors coming into the hospital? Why would anyone do that?" For some reason Thatcher thought she knew but wasn't sure enough to share it yet. "And you have an idea that the board members are keeping it for some reason?"

"Yes, but I don't know why. It's not been tampered with. It's all there, all accounted for. Even the money that the children raised for their school is there. And that would be the first amount that I'd think would be missing. It's small and has no earmarks on it, such as a corporation donation." She moved the curser around again. "I'm going to have to do this at home. It's too much for this little thing. So, I was going to ask you, if the hospital does close down, what will you do? I mean, you're a fantastic doctor, and I'm sure that there are people out there that would want you to come work for them."

"Are you trying to butter me up for something? If you are, I need details before I answer that." He knew she was going to ask him to stop working, and that broke his heart. He loved what he did and wanted to do it forever. "What did you have in mind?"

"The agency that I work for is forever trying to find good qualified doctors that can and will work under cover. Say one of us were to get hurt, or someone that we're after. It happens sometimes, that we don't mean to have them killed but they are. I really do know what they do at my job, I'm not stupid. I just don't like to think about it." He asked her if she was kidding. "Absolutely not. Donaldson asked me to talk to you because his boss asked him to do it. And that would be another person that you'd have to help out if needed."

"You mean someone like the president?" Thatcher was joking, but Rogen wasn't. "I can't work for the president of the United States. That's just.... Well, I don't know what that is."

"I work for him. Indirectly of course, but he signs my paychecks, along with a few other people's that aren't military. Winnie isn't, but Donaldson is, believe it or not." She pulled out an envelope and told him some of the perks he'd enjoy. "When he goes on vacation, you do. It's always someplace nice. And when he leaves office you have the say so if you stay with the incoming president or not. The money is great. You'd make more than me."

"I've been meaning to ask you about that. You put me on all your accounts. What does that mean?" Rogen cocked a brow at him. "I know what putting me on your accounts means. But what accounts are you talking about?"

"I have some nice property in two other countries. I have big investments that you share with me. Also, I have a nice 401k that will keep us in money. And since I'm forever on the computer, I know when and where to move my money. Our money." He asked her how much, ball park. "Just over one billion. Could be more because I've not had time to check it since we got married."

He drove the rest of the way just answering her questions. Thatcher was having a hard time wrapping his mind around how much money she had. Not that he was a snob or anything. But she had a great deal more than he did. Then he let it go. Money doesn't mean anything if you don't have someone that you love. Sappy, he thought, but it was about right.

"This job that you're talking about. Will I have insurance? Like malpractice insurance? That's pretty high for me now. I can't imagine that I'd be able to pay that if something happened to the president." She laughed. "You were kidding me, weren't you?"

"Not at all. I was thinking that only a doctor would worry about something like that." He didn't understand and she laughed harder. "You'll have a car and a jet at your disposal. Every new thingamajig that you need or even want. You won't have to wear a uniform or whatever you call that baggy stuff you wear. Which is very unsexy if you ask me." She laid her head on the seat and looked at him as she continued. "The most important thing you'll have, which makes me feel better, is round the clock security, as will your parents and brothers. That's in the event someone gets it in their head that they can kill him off — the president, I mean — by holding your family hostage."

"Where did the money come from that you set up for the pack?" She frowned at him. "My head is making the circuit around things I wanted to talk to you about while trying hard not to think of this job offer. Where did it come from? You?"

"Yes. And you, if you want to be technical. There is no point in letting the pack fail when it was easy enough for me to put the money in there to help out." He asked her why she didn't tell Shane. "What would you do if you found out that he had put money in your account so that you could keep afloat?"

"Good point. All right. Next question. Why did you save the Conrad family? Yes, you were in the right place at the right time, but I think it was more than that. What was it, if you don't mind me asking?" She looked out the front window; they were nearly home now. "You don't have to tell me, Rogen."

"The little boy, Levi. Every morning when there was school, he'd wave at me. Like it was something that he'd been practicing for days. And he always had a smile on his face. A couple of times, he had one of the babies wave at me too. It touched something deep inside of me that hadn't been touched for a while. Tenderness." He told her that he loved her. "And I love you. Would you like to have a baby or two with me?"

"Yes. Very much so. I'd love to have as many as you want. One or two dozen, I don't care." She told him she'd work up to twenty-four children. "Good. I love you very much, Rogen. I don't think I tell you that nearly enough."

Chapter 10

There were hundreds of people at the funeral. Lisha looked around twice to make sure that Jimmy's was the only service being held today. And so many people came up to her, wishing her well and giving her condolences. She didn't know any of them. Not one person except Thatcher's family and her son and daughter.

When there was a lull in the line of people, she went in search of Rogen. She was beautiful in her long black skirt and blood red blouse. Lisha had thought it would be tacky to wear to a funeral, but her daughter was not only able to pull it off, but Thatcher had a tie on of the exact same color. They looked like a wedding cake topper.

"Mom, are you all right?" She looked at her son. Jamie was as good looking as Thatcher was handsome. She shook her head when he asked again. "Do you need me to get you a drink of water?"

"No. I'm just overwhelmed, I guess." He took her hand, the first time since she'd been living in the house with them that he'd shown any sort of affection toward her. "I don't know these people. Why are they here?"

"Some of them are people that I've worked with. But I think most of them are friends of Thatcher's. He's a good man, don't you think?" She said that she liked him. "I do too."

Jamie had taken her out to his barn just this morning. He'd not wanted to, she could tell, and was reluctant to go with him. But Thatcher said it was a good thing he was doing, showing his mom his job, and Jamie changed his attitude just like that. Oh, to have had that kind of effect on either of them, she thought. A friendly conversation that didn't end in her crying all the time.

The barn was filled with equipment that she'd never heard of before. But Jamie had not only shown her around the big cavernous place, but he also showed her how some of the equipment worked. There were two pieces that he'd not been able to run for her, as Thatcher told him he need more practice. Then he showed her his art.

"I never knew you were so talented. My goodness, Jamie, these are amazing." He was embarrassed by her praise, but she didn't think he'd be mad. "Where did you learn to do this? It must take you hours to get just one of them done."

"Sometimes when Rogen was working on assignment, she sent me to this nice school around the corner from where we lived. It was really fun, and I asked if I could go all the time." He showed her his very first piece. "It's not all that good. Not like I can do now."

"I think it's lovely." She looked up at her son when he said her name, tearing her out of her memory of earlier. "I'm sorry. I was thinking of something else. What did you say?"

"I asked you if you wanted to have a seat. The service is about to begin." She was escorted to the front by Thatcher. Jamie had to be ready to be a pallbearer. Thatcher sat her down next to Rogen, then sat by her.

The service wasn't that long. The minister didn't know Jimmy — few people here did, she supposed — but it was nice, the things he said. He even told about how he'd come to see his children for the last time but hadn't made it. He died trying to tell them that he loved them. That was when he went into making sure you live everyday as if it were your last. Lisha thought that was good advice, and she was going to make sure she did that as much as she could.

As they were leaving the church, Lisha thought about the other funeral home that she'd gone to with Rogen. The man had been rude and nasty, and it wasn't until Rogen stood up to take her someplace else that she realized that he was treating her like white trash. They were nearly to the car when Rogen said she'd forgotten her purse and went back in to get it. It wasn't until they were riding to the next place that she realized that Rogen hadn't carried a purse.

"What did you do to that man?" Rogen grinned and said she'd done nothing. "I don't believe you. What on earth did you do to him? Rogen, you didn't kill him, did you?"

"No. Not yet at any rate. But he'll never treat anyone like he did us again. I made sure of that. The nerve of that fucking bastard." The driver laughed and Rogen joined him. "This place we're going now is the church that is on pack land. Shane offered it to us when we told him about Dad's death. He said it was large, and he even told us that we could bury Dad back there. You too when the time came. This way, you can visit him anytime you like."

"I'd like that." Rogen had nodded. "Rogen, Mrs. Robinson, she said it would be her pleasure to teach me how to read. I talked to her last evening. And she's nicer to me now too. I wasn't all that nice to her when we first met. I wasn't nice to a lot of people, including you and Jamie."

"You were fine, Mom. It was us. And I'm not going to tell you that we didn't deserve to be rude, but we should have taken your feelings into consideration more than we did." Lisha said nothing. "Thatcher said he found a buyer for the camper. And he's going to buy the truck from you to use."

"Thank you for that. I just don't think I could use it on my own. Too many memories." She looked out the window and the lovely little church they were in came into view. "Oh Rogen. It's perfect. Just like a picture. Thank you for bringing me here after me putting up such a fuss about the other place."

"I had no idea that he'd be a jackass, but I had heard that he was a prick. I'll take care of him too." She didn't know what that meant and was positive that she didn't want to. Rogen was good at whatever she did, and that was all she knew. "Mom, are you all right?"

For the second time in the last few hours, she'd been pulled from her memories. Vowing to pay attention from now on, she walked with Thatcher on one side of her and Rogen on the other. Once they were standing near the open grave, Thatcher went to the hearse to be a pallbearer with Jamie. Sitting in the chair offered to her, Lisha watched as her husband, her friend, was brought to his final resting place.

There were nice words being said, Lisha was sure. But all she could think about was that she was alone now. No more would Jimmy be there with her when she was watching television. He'd not be around to help her with small things around the house. There would be no more plans for the future for the two of them. The trip to Florida was finished.

Leaning on Rogen's shoulder, she told her that she loved her and Jamie. Loved them for taking her in, for giving her peace, and most of all for accepting her when she needed them most. Jamie handed her a tissue, then hugged her too. Lisha felt something that she'd never felt before—love from her children. Something that she was positive she did not deserve.

Going back to their home, Lisha sat at the table, just watching the people that had come there. There were a great many of them that were well dressed, some of them in military uniform. And all of them seemed to know Rogen.

She was delightful, Lisha noticed. Friendly to everyone. Hugged a great many of the men and women alike. Some of the people were introduced to her, but Lisha knew that she'd never remember their names. And it was doubtful that she'd see them again.

When Maggie sat next to her and put a plate of food in front of her, Lisha started to shove it away. She didn't think she could eat, ever again.

"No, you don't, young lady. You eat something. I'll talk, you'll listen. I was thinking about something that I think you might be on board with. I have a place in town that caters to some of the handicapped veterans that come home. Some of them are damaged physically, a lot of them emotionally. There are even a few of them that I worry won't be able to come back from where they've been." Lisha opened her mouth. "Unless you're putting food in there, you close that mouth of yours right now. I'm talking."

"You're very rude, aren't you?" Maggie laughed, and Lisha couldn't help but join her. "I guess it works when you have six boys running under foot. Jimmy and I, we wanted more children. For all the wrong reasons. But these two—while I had nothing to do with them being what they are, I'm very proud of them."

"You should be. And don't cut yourself short. Had you

been a better parent, then maybe they'd not have turned out like they did. Yes, I'm rude, but I don't beat around the bushes when I have something to say. You've come a long way, Lisha. I didn't want to like you, but you've turned me around." Lisha thanked her. "You're so very welcome. Now, I want you to come and help me out at the veterans' offices. It'll do you good to see people that are suffering more than you. Get you to realize that there is more to life than grief."

"Have you ever lost anyone?" Maggie nodded and looked away. "I'm so sorry. That was really mean of me. I'm sorry."

"My parents. They were tigers too, as you can guess. They'd been captured by some very bad men, and they... they killed them horribly. Then they skinned them. I wasn't very old, maybe twelve or so, but for a long while I didn't trust humans at all. I wanted nothing at all to do with any of them. They'd all killed my parents, was my thinking." Lisha asked what had turned her around. "That man over there. My Thatch. He's the best thing that could have happened to me. And I just don't know what I'd do without him with me. I can't feel your pain of the loss of a husband, but I do hurt for you. And want to help you."

"I'll have to think about it. I mean, I feel so fuddled right now." Maggie said that she understood that. "Thank you, Maggie. You've been wonderful to me and my children. Jamie cannot say enough great things about the two of you. He said you take him to dinner out all the time. I've never been anywhere but a fast food place. It's easier to read the menu there."

"I have a girl's day out, and you'll come with me." She started to tell her that she wasn't up for that. "We do it once a month, and when the weather is nice, we have teas in someone's flower garden. You'll get to meet women of your own age as well as have some fun. Do you want anything else?"

Lisha looked at the now empty plate. Then she looked up at Maggie. With a wink, the woman slipped away and left her there. She did feel better, she thought. Having just a little food on her belly made her feel like she could do this.

Getting up, she walked around the room and let people talk to her. At first, she was nervous. Then the more she did it, the better she felt about it. As she was talking to a gentleman, Rogen came up to stand beside her and hugged the man. Lisha couldn't for the life of her remember his name.

"Leave my mom alone, you old letch." The man laughed. "I didn't think you'd be able to come here, Mr. President. My family and I thank you—"

"You're the president?" The man laughed and told her that he was. "I'm so sorry. I feel so stupid. I had no idea who—I'm so sorry. I feel so foolish."

"No reason to feel that way, Mrs. Hall. You have a great deal on your mind, and you just lost your husband. When my wife passed away, I could barely get out of the bed. You're going much better than I was. And I want to thank you for just being you." She asked him what he meant. "You were talking to me as if we were old friends. I don't get that a great deal in my line of work. I do hope you'll come and visit me sometime when I have to see Rogen. She's my best man, and there isn't anyone that I trust more than her. You did a fantastic job with both your children."

She started to tell him that she'd not been a good parent at all when Rogen cut her off. "My mom is going to be staying with us until we can find her a house. But she won't be far away. I think that'll be wonderful for us when we have children."

Lisha let them talk, thinking that Rogen was either embarrassed about her or she didn't want the man to know. When he walked away, hugging them both and telling them once again that he was sorry, Rogen turned her to look at her.

"I'm neither embarrassed or whatever else is running through your mind. You did make us what we are. And when someone says that to you, you simply say 'Thank you. I did, didn't I?' We're starting over, Mom. We don't have to bring up the past anymore. I'd like for us to move forward from now on, and not think about the past." She nodded, her eyes and heart so full then. "Mom, I'm sorry. About everything. But I'm serious. We need to move on. All right?"

"Yes, that's fine with me. I'd like that."

Rogen hugged her and took her around the room. So many people, her mind kept saying, and all for her children. It hit her then that she was exhausted, that the food had made her sleepy.

"Rogen, do you think I could go lie down? I haven't been sleeping all that well."

She was helped up the stairs to the room she'd been staying in and laid down. Lisha only had one thought before sleep took her under, and it was that she was home. For the first time in her life, she felt like she was home.

~*~

Rogen was still doing research on the hospital when she found something that wasn't adding up. In order to find what the key was, Rogen broke into one of the emails from the hospital board and found the answer to a great many things. Getting up and dancing around the room, she turned when Thatcher asked her what she'd found.

"The key to the jackpot. The reason nothing is being paid." Rogen showed him the email from a bigger firm inquiring about the sale of the hospital. And when it would come to fruition. "They're making it look worse than it is. I'm not sure why yet, but I'll figure it out. I mean, if I was going to sell off a hospital like this one, I'd want it to be worth more, wouldn't you?"

"Not necessarily." She asked him why not. "Because there is a profit sharing with the place. It was put in place right after I did my internship. Every time we make a profit on something, even small things, like saving gloves that cost, sheets that need to be replaced, we get money back once a year. If there is no profit—which there never seems to be—then the money that is left over is for the board and their time. Otherwise, they don't get anything much for helping the hospital."

"That's just stupid. Why would they save that money instead of getting more for the hospital in the long run?" Then it hit her. "You'd get a part of that too. A profit off the sale. What a slimy piece of shit. So, if they sell a falling down hospital, they would come out more ahead than they would from the sale of a profit making one. And all the money that isn't used for the things that you guys need, it goes to the board. That fucking sucks—you know that, don't you?"

"Yes. But I never thought of it until you told me about the sale. I should have remembered that. But we haven't gotten any profits for—I don't know, the last five years or so. It used to be five figures for doctors and less for nurses. I would usually split mine up with my operating room staff." She told him that was nice. "Yes, but it's hurt them the last few years. I think some of them were depending on that for things like Christmas and such."

She sat back down at the computer and was still looking at what she could find when Thatcher started to rub her shoulders. She loved him for this. It wasn't until he started to massage her that she realized how tense she was.

"How about we take your mom to the houses we have lined up, and then come back here and chase each other in the woods?" She moaned. "I have to tell you something. If we don't have sex at least four times a day, I might just die."

"You're a goof." She got up and turned to him. "I think, sir, that is an excellent idea. And after we chase each other around, how about we come in the house and have some major sex in our room?"

"Yes." Thatcher kissed her then, working his mouth all the way down to her throat. There he bit her, and she could have sworn he'd shocked her with a high voltage wire. "If we keep this up, your poor mother is going to—"

Thatcher cursed like a man on leave. As he was pulling out his phone to answer it, she thought that their plans were done. It was the hospital calling, and he'd have to leave. And when he said he'd be right there, she knew it.

"I have to go." She said she understood. "I know you do, but that doesn't make me any less pissy about it. I tell you what. You take your mom to the house, and if I can, I'll meet you at one of them and we can still have fun."

She kissed him goodbye and hated to see him go. But after telling Mom that she was ready, they made their way to the car, both of them seemingly in a sour mood.

"I was so hoping that Thatcher could come with us." She asked her mom why. "Well, this person is more than likely going to think that he can take us to the cleaners, and you'll have to kill him. I just don't want to have to explain how stupid the man was for underestimating my daughter." Then she got into the car, like she'd not just made a huge joke.

Still laughing, Rogen got into the car and asked her if

she'd like for a witness to come along with them. Mom told her that would be good, just to be sure their side was heard.

"I don't know what got into you today, but you should be loosened up like that more often. I tell you what. We'll go by and see if Thatch can go with us, and he'll be a good source of entertainment for us too." Mom said that was great. "You really are going to live close, right? I mean, you're not going to decide to go back to your home?"

"Would that bother you if I did?" Rogen didn't even hesitate but said it really would. "I'm not. But I do thank you. Besides, there is nothing left there. The house and the entire street was being torn down as we were leaving town. Nothing is there. Just memories that I'd just as soon not think about. I plan on making new ones. And happy ones."

Thatch was more than happy to go with them. Maggie was fussing at him about the mess he'd made in the kitchen, and he wanted to avoid her for a bit. He asked if they could make one stop on the way home.

"I need to get her flowers. I messed up big time. But I had no idea how to make the coffee pot thing work. I had no idea it took poddlings, or whatever they're called." Mom corrected him. "Pods. Still. I thought the hole there was mighty small for coffee to make a pot."

Rogen was still giggling about it when they pulled up in front of the first home. Immediately, she hated it. There was something very ugly about it. Flowers surrounded the porch and there were pretty trees in the yard, but Rogen hated it on sight.

"Do we have to go in?" Rogen looked at her mom. "I don't want to live in a house that looks like the one we had before you left."

Rogen looked at the house, and it dawned on her why

she disliked the house so much. Mom was right. It was almost exactly like the one she'd grown up in. Thatch said he'd take care of it and went up to tell the realtor that they'd meet her at the next house. She was fine by that and led them to it.

Now this one, Rogen liked. The realtor was talking to Mom as Rogen walked around the living room. She could see her mom with a tree by the front window. A fire in the fireplace, as well as having her grandchildren over as she so desperately wanted. The big dining room would hold them if she were to have dinner, and the house had four bedrooms. All on one level so that Mom wouldn't have to worry about stairs later in life.

"This is about perfect for her." She told Thatch that she agreed. "I was thinking too that Maggie and I, we'd be more than happy to help her out with her new appliances and such. Just for her turning a corner, so to speak."

Rogen kissed him on his head. Thatch was a wonderful man, and she loved Maggie to pieces. Thatcher had been very lucky growing up with them in his corner.

Her mom came around the corner with a look of absolute terror on her face. Before she could ask her what had happened, she was handed a paper. It told about the house, what was new and used, and how many acres it was. Rogen didn't want to embarrass her mom. Thatch took the hint and asked the realtor if she'd come with him to see the yard. Give the ladies time to talk.

"It's fine, Mom. I have it." She asked her what it said. "It's just a sheet telling about the house, when it was built, as well as all the appliances you'll need to get. You have five acres, which means that Thatcher and I can come here on a run if we want. And there are the makings of a garden in the back. You'd like that, wouldn't you?"

"I love this house, Rogen. It's within walking distance to your home if you need me. I can go to the store, too, in the other direction from the house. And I'd love to have a garden to play around in." Rogen told her that she liked it too. "Do you mind if we go to the basement? She was nice and all, but she talked too fast for me. Just show me the furnace and stuff. I don't know squat about it, but I'd like to see if it's rusty or not."

"Sure."

The furnace, according to the paper that she had, was brand new. There was a bit of water damage on one wall, but that could be fixed. The roof was only three years old, and there was a ceiling fan in each bedroom. Mom fell in love with the master suite.

"I've never had my own bathroom before." She squealed in delight when she saw the deep garden tub. "Why, I could soak in here for hours and watch the animals in the back yard."

Rogen made a mental note to ask some of the other shifters in the area to come by here once in a while so that Mom could have a nice view. They were headed back to the kitchen when Thatch came in with the realtor.

"I've been working her down on the price, Lisha. I told her how your husband recently died and you're going to be moving here to be close to your daughter and son. She liked that." The woman, Rogen thought her name was Sally, agreed it was a lovely thing. "Sally here said that she'd take ten grand off the price, and throw in one of them homeowner's insurance packages."

Rogen looked at her mom and asked her what she wanted to do. There was one more house to see. Mom asked if she could walk around once more alone. When they all agreed to wait for her, Mom took a long tour of the house. Rogen told Thatcher what was going on.

That's wonderful, Rogen. And you told her that we're buying the house, didn't you? She told him not yet, but she would. *I'm glad she found something that she liked. And someplace where she could live by us. But, honey, I might be a little longer than I thought. There's been another shooting on one of the families from the pack. Have you found out anything yet?*

Yes. I'll talk to Shane and the police when we're done here. You're not going to believe who it is. He said he had to go but would talk to her later.

Rogen told Thatch what was going on. "I have to contact Shane and let him know so that he can tell me if he wants to take care of it himself or let the police handle it."

"Is it pack?" She shook her head and told him it was a human, as they'd thought. "Then telling Shane will be good, but he won't be able to take care of it himself. He'll want to, don't get me wrong, but he won't. Not with it being a human. You sure? Never mind. I know you are. You don't do a thing unless you're sure. All right. How about I call him to us. That way he can sniff out anything we might not see. Also, you might want to tell your mom that so long as you guys visit her often, she won't have any trouble with rodents."

Her mom told her that she really wanted this house. So, before Sally could tell her about financing and such, Rogen interrupted her. She had dealt with this sort of thing before.

"My husband and I will be paying cash for the house. But before we close, we'd like to have the carpets all cleaned and the garage out back to have the floors power washed. That way my mom won't have to worry about getting dirty when she uses it, all right?" Dollar signs were all she could see in Sally's eyes. "Also, and this is important for the sale to go through, my mom will need for you to make sure that the homeowner's insurance is up to date. A house this old, she might have a few issues."

"Yes, we can do that. I can get started on the carpets right away. When will you be moving in, Mrs. Hall?" Mom said as soon as possible. "Then I'll call my boss now and have him get a start on this. I'm probably not supposed to tell you this, but you are my first home buyer. Thank you so much. I can't believe it. Thank you."

She and her mom stopped by the furniture store on the way home. Rogen had a list of things she would need, as well as a list of things that she and Jamie had had in the rental. When she saw her mom looking longingly at the new bedroom set, she tossed the used list away, and they had a wonderful time buying for her new home.

Chapter 11

Thatcher wanted to be in on both the meetings that Rogen had set up. One of them was with the Feds, who were at the hospital with Rogen, and he was here with the local police taking care of the person who had, so far, murdered three people. All of them pack.

"Mrs. Bundy, we have a warrant for your arrest." The mayor, her husband, looked at them and laughed. He asked if Tommy had sent them. "No, sir. We're here to arrest one April Bundy for the attempted murder of the Conrad family, and for the murder of Phil Jenkins and his wife, Patty Jenkins."

"This is absurd. What is this really about? You there, Robinson? Is this your idea? Coming here at election time to make sure that I lose? Is that it?" Thatcher had been warned to keep his mouth shut. "You can't be accusing my wife of killing anyone. Just look at her. She'd not hurt a fly."

He was here for Rogen and that was all. However, he was not only armed, but he was also wearing a vest that had *Police* written on it to keep his upper body safe. So he stood there, keeping his mouth shut, but wondering about why Mayor

Bundy would think this had anything to do with him.

"Your wife, sir, has been seen carrying out the murder of Mr. Jenkins and his wife. She had them pull over, and then she pulled a gun on Mr. Jenkins. After making sure he was dead, checking his pulse to make sure, April then shot and killed his wife, Patty."

"There isn't any way anyone saw me do anything." Thatcher tensed up. He wasn't sure, but he thought that she'd just admitted that she'd kill them. "Besides, this world would be a much better place if not for those monsters that shift into other beings. Why, you would think that I'd done something wrong by killing them. It's my duty as a Christian to make sure that the world is clean of such things."

"Mrs. Bundy, are you admitting that you killed these people? I want to warn you, we have on body cameras, and they're recording every word you say. Don't you want an attorney?" April waved him off and asked the maid to get some tea for everyone. "No, thank you, ma'am. I'd like for you to come down to the station, please. We have some questions that we need to ask."

"I just told you that I'm a Christian and that I was doing right by the city. My goodness, man, have you seen how they are in our schools? In our churches? It's an abomination to have them around. No, I'm not going anywhere. And if you were half the policeman that you should be, then you'd agree with me in having them all murdered in their beds. All the women are breeding more of those little creatures to grow up and become the same monsters that their parents are. Sucking all the life out of our God fearing community like they have a right to." She thanked the maid politely and took a sip of tea. "Come sit down. We'll discuss the next round of genocide for these people. If we could gather them all in one place, all of them at once, we can poison the food that they have at their meetings and be done with the lot of them. Come, have a tart. They're very good."

Her maid, Lillian, was still standing behind her and Mrs. Bundy turned to look at her. When she asked her what she was wanting, April turned back to them, sipping her tea, eating a tart like nothing was insanely wrong.

"Mrs. Bundy, I'm a shifter too. Do you wish me dead?"

Instead of answering her, April Bundy pulled out a gun from the side of her chair and shot her maid right in the head. As she fell to the floor, brain and other matter spraying out behind her, April turned to her husband.

"You'll have to put an ad in the paper, dear. I need a maid that can be trusted, and one that isn't one of those shifter monsters." No one moved. Mayor Bundy finally slid to the floor, his face as white as the snowy covered blanket that rested on the back of the couch. "Why are you all just standing around? We need to plan. We need to get busy. My God, gentlemen, do I have to do this all on my own?"

"Mrs. Bundy, you are under arrest for the murder of Lillian Parker. There are other charges too, but right now I'm so shocked that I can barely believe you just did that. And in front of the police." She asked him what was it he felt like she'd done. "You pulled out a gun and murdered her. No reason at all, you just killed her."

"So I did. And you should be thanking me, not treating me like I'm some sort of — I don't know — criminal. Once I get this mess taken care of, we'll talk. Let me call Lillian— No, no, can't do that. She's moved on. How about I just throw something over her for now and we'll plan?"

Andrew moved forward slowly, telling April her rights as he did so. Mayor Bundy stood up but stayed out of the way. Nothing like having your own wife kill someone in front of you to make you aware of what she'd been doing. April pulled out her gun again and fired.

"Are you all right?" Thatcher looked up, and it took him a moment to realize it was his mom. He leapt to his feet and hugged her tightly. The morning hadn't gone well, he told her, and she held him while he poured out the entire story.

"She pulled out her gun the second time and fired at Andrew. Just like it was her duty to do so. And had the mayor not moved in front of her gun, she would have killed him. As it was, she shot her husband in the head and he just dropped to the floor with Lillian. She had two children, Mom. Who is going to look after them now?"

"There, there, son. It's all right. I have you now." He nodded, watching the first body bag coming out of the house. He didn't know who it was—it could have been any of the three of them. "Where is April now, son? I do hope she's getting taken care of too."

"She's dead as well. When she shot her husband, she simply put the gun to her head and killed herself. It was a bloody nightmare. All that death over a group of beings that meant her no harm." Mom looked him in the face. He knew that he was covered in blood, and she asked him if he'd been hurt too. "No, this is from the mayor. When he stood in front of Andrew."

"I want you to listen to me. I've spoken to Andrew too. You clean yourself up and then get to the hospital with your mate. She knows that you're upset, and she can't reach you." He said he'd talk to her. "It won't do her a bit of good just to hear from you, Thatcher. You get to her. Do you hear me, Thatcher? She'll need to know that you are physically all right. Clean up. Dad has clothing in the car for you. I'm sorry it's not a suit, but you go now."

He did. Cleaning up was harder than he thought it would be, and he had to be hosed down with the coldest water he could stand. Then after dressing in a pair of tear-away pants and a shirt, Dad gave him his jacket and Thatcher got a police escort to the hospital where Rogen was. Running up the stairs instead of taking the elevator, he met her on the stairs.

"You bastard." She hit him between kisses. "You said you'd not get hurt if you went with them. You promised me that."

"I didn't get hurt, honey. I promise. But I did scare you, and for that I'm so sorry. And I'm going to do some things to make it up to you. As soon as possible. I've decided that I'm taking a long vacation with you. Just us three going to places unknown for a month." He kissed her again. "I'm so sorry, love. I've been gone more than here in the last few weeks. I was late coming home last night, then had to go out early this morning for another surgery. Then this. I need some downtime with you and Jamie."

"Yes, all right. Anything. But not with Jamie. He's decided to live with Mom for a while. The two of them are going to take a trip. But not in a camper. This is to get to know her, help her with her studies." Thatcher knew that Jamie was going to ask his mom if he could; he was just surprised that Lisha was going to want it. "I think they'll be all right, don't you?"

"Yes, more than all right. Not just for him, but for her too. I think—no, I believe that she's changed since driving here. Her and your father both. It's only too bad that you didn't get to hear it from him. Did you read the letter yet?"

"Not yet. I was going to when I get home today." Good, he thought. He also wanted to ask her about the thumb drive but decided that he could do that too when they got home.

Climbing the stairs to the fourth floor, he certainly hoped this went much better than his meeting. Of course, he thought, they were at a hospital this time.

There were several people in the room that he knew — a lot more that he didn't. His father was there, but he wasn't sure why until he asked him to fix his tie.

"You sure made good time, Dad." He flushed brightly. "What are you all dressed up for? You headed someplace after this?"

"No, I've got it in my head that I can do a damned sight better running this place than they did. You think I can do it?" Thatcher told him he'd be a shoe in. "Yes, well, I might need you to vote or something for me. Dawson said he might, but he'd have to think on it. I swear, that boy gets more smart assed every time I see him." They both laughed. "But son, I really think I can do this. I have the smarts for it."

"You do. Never doubt that, Dad. You're the only person I know, besides Mom, that can raise six boys on what little you made each week, and still have some money left over for important things, like life with us." Dad smiled at him. "I love you, old man."

"And I love you very much, dick head."

They'd been saying the same thing to each other since Dad and he had watched a movie about this sheltered young man. It was the first time he'd heard his dad laugh so hard that he had tears in his eyes afterwards. But he never said anything like that around Mom.

The door opened behind him and he turned when everyone else did. It was the three board members. They had planned a meeting this afternoon, but it wasn't going to go as they had thought it might. The man in charge, Agent Carl Jamison, asked Elizabeth Slone, Cartwright Phillips, and

Donald Wind to have a seat.

"I'm sorry, but we've booked this room for a conference call out of state. You'll have to wait until we're finished here." Elizabeth looked at him. "Thatcher? What are you doing here? Shouldn't you be cutting costs in your department? I would think that a man with time on his hands would be better served in trying to keep his job."

"Are you threatening me?" She just waved him off. "I asked you a question, Elizabeth. Are you threatening me about my job?"

"While I don't know who any of these other people are, I won't air out dirty laundry here. So, if you'd like to set up a meeting with me tomorrow, I'll talk to you. Until then, be on your way and take your little friends with you." She sat down, fully expecting, Thatcher thought, for him to comply with her wishes. "Well?"

"Well, what?" She huffed. It was cute really, but only because he knew what was coming next. "I think I'll stick around for the show."

The conference phone rang, and Cartwright answered it, telling the man on the other end to hang on a moment, they had company. He'd only gotten out a word or two before he was cut off by Donald. He told him again to hold on, they had company.

"I'm sure you do, you fucking bastard. Is it the FBI? The police and whatever else these people with letters on their jackets are with? You fucking bastard, you told me that this was a done deal. That the hospital was losing money every fucking day. And now that I've wasted all my time on trying to get you to deal with me, I find out that you're all going to prison."

Dawning hit all three of the board members at once.

Thatcher laughed. It felt good to be on the other end of their comments and snide remarks about him taking things home with him. Wasting the hospital inventory.

"You really didn't think you'd get away with this, did you? I mean, the hospital is more profitable now that I'm in surgery, a place that you didn't want me to be. You said that I was too flamboyant. Too much of a hot dog. I was never sure what you meant by those remarks, but I have a few for you three. Thief. Embezzler. Liar. And here's one that is perfect for summing it all up. Convicts."

~*~

As soon as they were in their room, Thatcher went to take a shower. He had told her about what had happened at the mayor's house, and she didn't blame him at all. But she needed him. Not just sexually, though that would help, but she wanted him to hold her. It had been a long day so far, and she wanted him to touch her.

"You scrub my back and I'll scrub yours." She smiled at him. "You're incredibly beautiful, did you know that? I love the way your hair is all mussy when you wake in the morning. The way all those curls seemed to be straining to corkscrew all up again when it's wet. I'm in love with the way that your waist seems to slide down into your hips with the curves of a sexy woman." She kissed him hungrily. "You didn't scrub my back, love."

"I have something else to scrub, thank you very much." She reached to his front after turning him around. Rogen's hands were soapy, his cock hard and slick now. Touching him this way was a treat for her. He couldn't touch her and hurry her along. "You are so full, I can feel you just wanting to release. Would you like for me to help you with that?"

When he turned around, Rogen went to her knees in front

of him. He handed her a large soft sponge to kneel on and she did that now. Taking his cock into her mouth, Rogen couldn't help but moan. He was hard, thick, and all hers.

"With you like this before me, it's all I can do not to come all over you. Just pull from your mouth and spray my cum on your body and face." She moaned again when he started to move. Rogen noticed too that he was holding onto the wall, the other hand gripping the nozzle tightly. "Rogen, please, let me come on you."

She pulled from his cock and opened her mouth to him. The water was hitting mostly the floor now. Rogen hadn't even noticed it being turned that way. And when the first hot stream of his cum hit her in the face, without anyone touching her, she came with him, screaming out from the release that startled her as much as it felt wonderfully fulfilling.

When he jerked her up from the floor, Thatcher slammed her body to the wall of the stall, his cock so quickly sliding into her that she came twice more even before he moved. Her breasts were abused by his mouth. His teeth grazed her throat, and all she could think about was the climax that was building up. The way her body seemed to be stretching toward some unknown finish line that she needed to reach first. And when Thatcher bit down on her throat, she did come.

But to call it something so mundane as that was a gross understatement, as it had her holding onto Thatcher's shoulders, digging her heels into his tight waist so that she'd not float away. And as soon as Thatcher came, filling her with his hot seed, Rogen just blinked out. Like he'd stabbed her right into her heart.

When she woke, he was beside her, his eyes closed in what seemed to her as a peaceful sleep. Looking at the clock, she knew that when it said that it was two, it was two in the morning and they'd slept through dinner again.

Getting up so as not to disturb Thatcher, she showered and dressed. The note that he'd left her on the counter said that he'd gotten called in last night again and didn't get home until just before eleven. Leaving the room, she let him sleep and headed to her offices.

The phone ringing an hour or so later made her realize that she'd not eaten much. Tossing away the nutrition bar wrappers, Rogen answered the phone. It was Donaldson.

"I have two questions for you. One is personal, so I'll leave that until last. Can you please look up something for me? An address on the street view." She pulled the place up he asked her about. "Do you see anything wrong with this place? Something that the rest of us here cannot see?"

"Such as?" While he asked someone else for a list, she began searching the exterior of the house. She found a camera on the front porch and hacked her way into that. It was then that she found out the entire house was wired. "The house is one I can look inside of as well. I don't have the connection as yet. Tell me what you need."

"I need you inside the house. But before you do that—" Rogen told him it was too late. "I'm so sorry, Rogen. I did mean to warn you first. Are they...honey, are they all dead?"

Rogen always tried to detach herself from what she looked at for the government. There had been times when it had been impossible for her to see anything more than they did. But this time, she was seeing it all. And there hadn't been time to isolate herself from the bodies that were present. Rogen was going to be professional about this even if it made her sick later. Pulling on her headset and hanging up her phone, she was speaking to the room Donaldson was in.

"There are four dead in the living room where I'm starting.

Two head shots, both male. One female, execution style. Hands tied to her front…legs? It looks like tape was used. The other woman, I can't tell — her face has been destroyed. Hands tied as well and her legs taped to the chair. Are there more in the house?" Donaldson said there were people missing. "Children?"

"Yes. Four of them. The SWAT team is on standby. No locals involved. There is also a group that you're familiar with just about four minutes away." There was no guessing time with Donaldson, he knew they were four minutes out. "Check all rooms on this floor, then the upper levels. If there is a basement, check it last."

The kitchen, dining room, as well as both powder rooms were clear. A great deal of blood in the kitchen, but no bodies. Rogen clicked on the cameras for the upper floors. Nothing in the hall, but there seemed to be as many as six more rooms up there.

"Master is clear, but someone was looking for something. I would say safe by the way they tore things off the walls. Floor is covered, but no ripped up carpet." She made her way to the next room — the nursery — and she had to breathe in and out before she could continue. "Nursery is clear, but the room has been trashed as well. Clothing torn from closet. There are two cameras in this room — the other shows that whoever came in shot a great many holes in the closet. Do you know if there is a panic room?"

"There is no mention of it, but that might be because it was added under private contractors. I'm checking that now." Rogen thanked him, her mind on auto pilot now. "It's in the sub levels. I'm hoping you can unlock it for me."

"I'll try. The next bedroom is clear. Two beds, two dressers, and a closet that has been done the same way as the baby's room. They seem to have wanted the children badly." Donaldson said something, but Rogen was breaking into the next camera. "This bedroom is clear as well. The closet and dressers are in worse shape as they're going along. I'd say that they're getting frustrated."

"Check the living room again. I have your team right outside the front door, and I want to make sure that they're going to be alone." Going back, she cleared it so that they could come in. They'd not make a noise since she was still searching the house. "They're going to stand where they are, Rogen. You tell me when you've finished."

The next two rooms had been destroyed. There was no other term for it. Beds were broken into splinters. There were gunshot holes all around the room this time. The dressers looked as if they'd been cut up with an axe. Rogen clicked into the last room on the floor.

"Bathroom, large, with a closet in the room. There is a woman there. Looks like a domestic. She's been raped if I'm seeing this right, and her throat cut. Donaldson, the presence of the domestic means the children were home, doesn't it?" She felt panic roll over her for the children. If she counted right, there were four children by the number of beds in the house. "I'm breaking into the basement. I need a minute. Just a minute."

"We don't know until you open the room for us if they're in the panic room. Just breathe, Rogen. You're doing a good job. Just breathe." She had an odd thought. Donaldson was a great deal nicer to her since he'd been dating Winnie. "Are you all right?"

"Yes." She looked up at Thatcher. He was wearing his jeans without the snaps done. His shirt was in his hand. She was sure that she'd frightened him and was glad for his company. "I have Thatcher here now. I'm doing better."

Breaking into the camera in the basement was easier. The rest of the codes had been the same, so she didn't think this one would be any different. Bad move, and she'd have to tell someone that it had probably helped the bad guys since they'd gotten in. She told the team to go down, the basement was clear.

"I need for you to bring in a rescue person, Tillson. I don't know that the children are in there, but they might need someone." Roger Tillson, one of her best men, said he had his medic with him. After thanking him, she zeroed all her efforts on the key lock on the large metal door. "I get one shot at this opening, so it might take me a minute or two to make sure I get it. It's been locked down. I'm betting by the domestic in the upper levels."

The program that she was using was written by her. She knew that it was possible that she could sell it off to the bad guys, but there was no reason for her to do that, not that she ever would. But she had enough money, support, and love now that little else mattered but helping people. When the program told her it had a match, she told the team to stand back, just in case it wasn't right.

"You think it'll blow?" She told Tillson that she didn't have any idea, but if it did, then it would be them and the house. "Good point. All right, we're back. Go ahead."

She coded in the key lock and waited. Rogen did wonder if she should have given someone there the code—it might have a remote lock out. But when her computer told her it was processing, she looked over at Thatcher.

"I want a baby in my arms. Someone that I can hold and cuddle after a day like this one is turning out to be. Soon. I don't care if it's ours or we raise someone else's. But I also want to have a child with you." He told her he was fine with that as well. "Guys, this is taking a long time. I'm worried."

"No worries. And if you want to have a child and don't care what kind of shifter it is, my sister is giving up her child for someone to raise. She's too young anyway." She asked about the father. "He's no longer a concern to anyone."

Rogen only looked at Thatcher, and he shook his head. Whatever had happened, she knew that if he wanted her to know, Tillson would tell her later. If not, then she'd be in the dark. It wasn't as if she couldn't dig around and find out what had come down, but she'd not do that. Not to him. Tillson, for all his bad boy vibes and the fact that he carried more weapons than a whole street of people might have, was a shy, funny man. She liked working with him too.

The lock disengaged and she held her breath as she watched the door swing open. It seemed to take forever, and she was sure that the children were all going to be dead. But when one of the men cried out that they had them, the cheers going up were loud and continuous. The four children of the house and the domestic's child were all unharmed.

Chapter 12

Morgan was in his office when he got a phone call. He was always tickled when he had to answer the old rotary phone. But then his office was one of the first ones built on the campus, and he loved to look out through the old bubbled windows that had stained glass pictures at the top of each one. Then he nearly fell off his chair when the dean, his boss, asked him if he had a few moments.

"Yes sir. Anytime for you." He meant it, of course, but he was worried that he sounded like a total suck up. "I'm just finishing up the paperwork for the next semester. I should have you a class itinerary as soon as the end of the week." Glancing at his calendar, he had to smile. It was only Monday and he could turn it in today, but he was going to make himself wait until Wednesday at the earliest.

After he turned off his laptop and locked up his office, he was nearly all the way to the dean's office when he thought of what he might be talking to him about. Christ, there had been that woman, kid really, who had wanted him to give her a higher grade for a little head. That's what she'd called it too, a little head. He liked to think that he was above average in that department, but thankfully, she'd never know.

His steps slowed when he saw that all the department deans were in the office. A small space like this one made it seem as if about two hundred people were in the room. But he was shoved inside and asked to have a seat. Morgan's mom had always told them, keep your mouth shut until you know the rules of the game.

Morgan felt the need to ask what he'd done, or even to explain about using too much paper on the copier. Even not finishing his meal the other day because he'd had to leave for the day. All kinds of things, most of them silly and not very trouble worthy, made their way not only through his thought process, but also to the tip of his tongue to tell on himself about.

Finally, Dean Sheppard cleared his throat.

"Jack Damion died last evening." He knew the man. Hated him too. Morgan and him would butt heads daily when the old geezer would find him in one of the halls. "I'd like to tell you he will be sorely missed, but I'm not going to lie to you, Morgan. You didn't like him any more than any of us did."

"No sir. He wasn't really willing to see my side of anything he cornered me on." He realized after he spoke that he shouldn't have. "I'm sorry. That was out of turn. He was a good man?"

Dean Sheppard laughed. "No, he wasn't a good man. Even before he bought his way into being on the board of deans, none of us cared for him." One of the men behind him cleared his throat. "If we're going to work with this young man, we need to have him telling us the truth when he knows it. Damn it, Jacobs, now you made me forget where I was."

"Working with you? Did you need me to take over his

classes? I have taken over several of them now, but I can squeeze a few more in if need be." Holliday laughed and said he was ever polite. "Okay, I'm already carrying his load with mine. But I enjoy the classes. It's sort of a change of pace for me to teach microbiology with finance added in for fun."

"No, it's not. He was a bastard for taking advantage of you. And to hear him tell it, he was doing you a favor. Something about you having too much idle time on your hands." The dean shook his head. "Deans are not required to teach any classes at this college. It's been that way from the beginning. When you're dean here, you spend your time getting to know the students, helping them out when they need it, as well as trying to come up with ways to raise money."

Dean Snow spoke from behind him. "I heard about that fundraiser your mother had. My goodness, it was nice to see all those teachers on the first day of class with all the supplies they'd need for the year." Everyone in the room nodded. "The fact is that sometimes we forget the teachers in the grade levels. And having all the supplies for them for the school year meant that the students didn't have to supply them. That was a capital idea."

"Thank you. Mom is very good at that sort of thing. My sister-in-law, Rogen, she's raised a bit of cash for the shelter and hospital that was badly needed." Another man talked a minute or so about the big to-do at the hospital and was glad that his brother Thatcher had been a part of that. "I'll tell him you said so. So, do you need me to ask my mom if she'll help you with one of the fundraisers?"

"No, no. You can, but that's not why we called you in here. We want you to fill the vacancy that Jack left open. You're a better man for the job anyway." Morgan didn't know what to say. Or if this was a joke. "Son, you're the man for the job.

We all voted on names last night when we found out about Jack. There wasn't a person in the room that said nay to you coming on board."

He didn't understand. It was like his brain had suddenly decided to freeze up and not comprehend what they were saying to him. When one of the others laughed, saying that he'd told them all that they'd leave him speechless, Morgan realized that it was a joke. Standing up, Dean Sheppard did as well.

"Morgan, this is no joke. I promise you that. I know your parents well enough that they'd hunt me down should I be tricking you this way. We want—we all want you to fill the vacancy left by Jack. Starting tomorrow morning." He put out his hand. In it was the silver and gold metal that would mark him with distinction. "As soon as we can get his office boxed up and sent to his family, we'd like for you to move into it. It's not much larger than the one you have now, but it's in a nicer place. You'd have a view from two sides of your office instead of just the one. The shelves are there for you to use—they're sort of a part of this old building, I guess. And there will be a set of keys given to you at the dinner we'll have in your honor."

There were more welcomes to their group. A great many pats on the back for him. Each man told him that it was an honor to be working with him, and they were so happy that he'd not turned them down. There were more congratulations given to him as well.

He was the youngest man there—he'd bet he was the youngest dean of studies ever brought into their group. Morgan was proud of himself. If he'd been alone then, he might well have given himself a pat on the back. Instead, he walked to his office that he had now and sat down in his chair.

He was a dean of higher educational studies. Holy Christ, his mom was going to shit. And his dad? He had no idea what he'd do, but he'd make a huge showing of having a son who was a dean. There were only two people ahead of him, besides the group of men he now worked with, and they were the president of the college and his vice president.

Picking up the phone to call his mom, he decided that he wanted to see their faces when he told them. So, instead of telling Mom what had happened today, he simply asked if they'd like to have dinner with him. In town.

"That would be lovely, son. Your dad and I were just talking about what to have. Where would you like to go?" He told her it was up to them, he was paying. He'd almost forgotten about the pay raise he was getting too. And perks. "Oh my, that is nice. Are you sure you have enough to make your bills if we go someplace nice?"

"Yes. I'm doing very well for myself, thanks in part to the work that Jonas has been doing for me." Christ, his mind kept skipping over things that had been said to him. "I was wondering, Mom, if you've given any plans of hiring yourself out as a person who organizes and plans fundraisers? Some of the professors here were just commenting on how well you did with the school supplies last year."

"I don't know, Morgan. I pretty much like to do it now because it's not something that I have to do. We'll talk on that more when we have dinner. I have to tell you, I'm excited about having dinner with the favorite second son." He laughed when she did. "I do love you, Morgan. Very much."

"I love you too, Mom."

He glanced down at the list that had been handed to him before leaving the offices today. He debated on telling his mom that he'd have a new number starting tomorrow but decided to wait. Just as he was hanging up, the movers came to box up his things to be moved. He didn't even have to pack his things up; that was a nice perk in and of itself.

Dinner was at his mom's favorite place. It wasn't expensive, but she loved it. The pasta dishes had always been her favorite, and Dad fell head over heels in love with the lasagna that they had. He also loved the desserts, and Morgan believed that he'd had all them at least ten times over the years since they opened.

"I have some news for you both. I wanted you to be the first to know." Dad asked him if it was bad. "No, not all of it. In fact, the little bit of bad weighs out— I've been made one of the deans of studies. Jack Damion passed away yesterday, and they asked me to be on the board with them."

Neither of them spoke. Morgan had never felt so disappointed in his life. And until his dad stood up and yelled whoopee at the top of his lungs, Morgan was sure that he'd made a mistake in thinking that they'd be happy for him.

The entire restaurant, including the staff in the front and back of the place, knew that he'd been promoted by the time the cheese was on their big bowl of salad. Other guests came by and told him congratulations, and the manager even brought them a bottle of wine. This was what he needed, Morgan thought. Family to boost him up when he needed it the most.

There wasn't a check for them to pay, so Dad, insisting on leaving the tip, left the waitress fifty dollars. He was a good man, and his pride in all of his sons showed through like this. Dad had celebrated for two whole days when Thatcher had become a surgeon and had done the same with the rest of them when they graduated from college. Morgan could only guess what he'd do for the next two days. Then he thought of what he'd done when Jonas had become owner of his own business.

"No taking out a full page ad in the paper, Dad." He looked so crestfallen that Morgan wanted to take it back. But Jonas had told him what a ribbing he'd taken around town for his dad's stunt. "You can put a little one in, no more than a half a page, but nothing more."

Dad's grin was infectious as they walked to their cars. Morgan hugged them both and told them his new number, as well as where he'd be located from now on. Mom asked him when he was going to tell the rest of the family.

"I hadn't thought of it, really. I mean, you two were the only two that I could think of when they offered it to me." He wasn't sure now that he'd ever said yes, but they must have assumed it—he did have keys. "What about at Sunday dinner? I mean, that'll be a good time to tell them all at once."

"Yes, that's a wonderful idea." Morgan looked at his dad, who was still pouting a little. "Thatch, behave yourself. You're making the boy wonder where the wood shed is."

"Dad, how about you tell them all on Sunday, instead of the big ad?" He didn't get a verbal answer, but Dad hugged him so tightly, he felt his belly rebel the food he'd just eaten. "Thanks, Dad. I love you too."

When they left him to go home and no doubt plan, he went to see how far along his office was of being packed up. It was finished. Walking across campus to his new place, not only were the boxes empty, but everything was where it had been before, in his old office. And he had an entire cabinet that was empty. He had his head stuck inside when someone knocked on his door.

Bumping his head, he went to the door. A little blood was on his finger, but it didn't worry him any. The kid standing there looked to be about twelve and was more interested in the blood on his fingers than he was in talking to Morgan. He asked if he could help him and put his hand behind him.

"Yeah. I'm looking for someone by the name of Damion." He told the child that he had passed last night. "Really? I have this letter here for him. It's special delivery. I'm the special delivery person at the post office. Now what do I do?"

"I don't know. But if you don't mind giving it to me, I'll make sure that someone in this office takes care of it for you." The kid looked undecisive. "You could call your boss if you'd like. Tell him I'm Morgan Robinson."

The kid only had to mention his name to his boss, apparently, and was given permission to leave the letter. It was shoved at him even as the kid was hanging up the phone. Morgan asked him for his name.

"Reed Morris. Thank you, sir. I really appreciate you helping me out."

Shutting the door behind Reed, he stuck the letter on his door. He'd remember it if it was there and decided that he'd had enough fun for one night. Morgan didn't think he'd fall asleep right away, but almost as soon as his head hit the pillow, he was out cold.

~*~

"I see." He was trying to wrap his head around the fact that Rogen had a sixty million dollar policy on her life, and he was going to get it if anything should happen to her. "It's a great deal of money, don't you think?"

"I'm important." She was laughing when she said that, but he knew how important she was. Not just to him, but to a few hundred people that she worked with, the president of the United States, as well as about two dozen people that worked in the main office who she guided into and out of trouble. "And the thumb drive—Winnie and I both have one of each of ours—is our last will and testament. We've never shared them with anyone before. At least I never have. But once you and I came together, I thought that I needed to fix mine for you. Winnie updates hers every year or so. I do as well. But this time, when we traded drives, she thought for sure that she was going to be killed. She had only fixed things on it that morning and made it so that Donaldson was her beneficiary."

"She keeps yours in a safe and you hers. Along with a copy of your own." Rogen nodded. "I don't understand why it is you're doing it this way and not just taking it to an attorney."

"I don't trust anyone with the knowledge of how much money I have. And who my insurance is with. Can you imagine what an attorney would do with that information if he wanted? I'd be dead before you could get me to the hospital." There was that. Thatcher looked at the sums of just property alone that she had gotten for herself. "I have money, so I don't need to work. Neither do you, for that matter. The house is paid for, and you can either take the job that the new board offered you or not. Just don't take it because it's a great deal more money. We don't need for you to work a job that you don't want."

"I do want it. There are perks with it too. I'd be home more through the evening. I won't have to work weekends unless there is an issue, or I'm needed for an emergency." He thought of the job he was taking. Physician to the president would have been quite a feather in his hat. But it would take him from his family, and he didn't want that. Being head of surgery at his current location would be something that he wanted more. Just to be able to spend more time at home and with the kids that would soon be coming along.

"You want to remain here? You're sure about that?" Thatcher felt a great weight off his shoulders as he nodded yes to Rogen. "Thank goodness. I wanted to support you all the way, but I didn't want you to be gone from me anymore than you have to. I love you."

"And I love you. When do we go to the hospital?" Rogen looked down at her notes. "And you don't mind raising a cougar, then?"

"No. I mean, a cat is a cat, I think. Sure, the little boy will be different from us, but we won't have to explain to him that we're shifters and such. Besides, I think this little guy will be perfect for this family. A lot of uncles to teach him how to have fun and chase the girls." She was still laughing when she looked down at her notes again. "We have to be there in an hour. I know she decided to come here to have him, but I want to go now and help her to hurry along."

"I've seen women in labor, love—you do not want to hurry her along if you can help it. And I'm sure that her being only fifteen, she'd be really snarly and nasty to you." Rogen got up off the bed they'd been sitting on. "You still think this is a good idea to not tell the family about him?"

"I do. What if she changes her mind? Or something happens to her? Tillson is very happy that we're going to raise him, but if something happens to his sister during this, he might change his mind." There was that. It had happened before when he'd been a resident. "Besides, I'd like to be able to do one thing that your parents don't know about until it's a done deal. My mom and brother are going to be there for tomorrow's dinner, so it'll be family time and the perfect time to spring a grandchild on them. Jamie will love being an uncle as well. Do you think your brothers will too?"

"Yes, and hell yes. I think that we'll have the best

babysitters in the world, and the child will be safe with them." He looked at her notes and saw that they still hadn't picked out a name. "You asked me what I wanted to name the baby. I think I have a name to put into the hat, if you're willing. James Thatcher Robinson. That was your father's first name, wasn't it?"

She nodded, her eyes filled with tears. He knew that it would be a perfect name for both parents, and he was glad that he'd looked up her dad's name. He'd gone by Jimmy for so long that even Rogen had had to look it up for her mom when she'd needed paperwork filled out.

The ride to the hospital was nerve-racking. They'd had to stop for a car seat and a diaper bag, so they'd left the house a little earlier than planned. Thatcher was nervous too, not having any idea what to expect. Yes, he'd held babies before, even delivered a couple. But they were going to be responsible for a tiny person, and he was a little overwhelmed.

The staff at the hospital knew him and Rogen, of course, so they took them aside and gave them both a gift. It was couple of bags filled with diapers, formula, as well as sleepers and other baby things. He was glad to see the sleepers. They'd completely forgotten to get clothing for little Jimmy.

The little girl was still in labor, so they sat in the waiting room, talking quietly. It wasn't but ten minutes later that Tillson — his first name was Roger — came to sit with them. He handed a blue folder to Rogen and spoke as quietly as they had been.

"That's all I have on the father of the child. I'm going to tell you what happened, but no one else knows or can know. She was raped, repeatedly, over a six day period. I haven't any idea how she conceived his child, but it matters little now. He was a member of my leap." Rogen asked him if he'd killed his family too. "No. I didn't have to. I would have, because they knew about it. Before he killed them, that is. He killed his mother then father so that he could have the bigger bed with my sister. Once she was able to get away, she told me who it was and what he'd done to her. She isn't doing well with having this child, I'll tell you that now."

"Is that why you and your wife didn't take him in?" Rogen knew a great deal about this man, and Thatcher liked him for his candor and his honesty. He didn't know what he would have done had it been his child or anyone else he knew. Roger told her that he had said he would, but his sister had said no.

"I mean, to the point she told us that if we did, she'd kill the baby and herself. She wanted no reminders of him." He handed her a second file. "Please put both of these in your safe. It's all the bloodwork and allergies that Angel has. Also, she wants no contact with him or you. She might change her mind later about seeing him, but I doubt it very much. Angel wants to move on with her life, and she can't do that if she thinks she might see him."

"How do you think that is going to work if we're neighbors?" Thatcher apologized for his tone. "I'm a little overwhelmed."

"It's all right, Thatcher. You've only had a few days to deal with this, I've had almost a year. But I have all the faith in the world in the two of you. I can't think of better parents for my nephew to go to." He looked down at his hands, then back at them. "At her request, my wife and I are sending Angel to a private school across the country. There no one knows her, and she can start her life over, so to speak. And before you ask why we didn't take him anyway, Angel made us promise. We can look in on him, but she does not want us to raise him. And really, after talking to a few doctors, I think her way is the smartest way."

"I'm so sorry for you, Roger. But you can come and visit him whenever you wish." Roger said that he might not, at first. "Anytime, I promise you. Is there anything you need from us? Besides raising up Jimmy as a good boy and wonderful man?"

"Jimmy. Believe it or not, my father's name was James. Is that his name?" Thatcher told him the full name. "That's a good powerful name, you guys. Thank you."

The nurse came back to tell them that Angel was in recovery and that their son was in the nursery getting cleaned up. Then she asked Thatcher if he'd like to come back and assist, with his wife. They both nearly knocked her down to get to him. As soon as he saw the little fellow in the nursery cart, he fell head over heels in love with the little guy.

"He weighed in at nine-pounds-six ounces. Twenty-one inches long and had a wonderful Apgar rating." Rogen asked her what that meant, and Nurse Kelly told her without being mean about it. "It's a test that was invented by Virginia Apgar, an obstetric anesthesiologist in nineteen fifty-two, to rate how a baby is holding up after being taken from his or her mother's womb. We take the test when the child is one minute old, and again at five minutes. Little Robinson here, he rated a five on both. Which is wonderful and means he's tolerating well."

When Rogen was allowed to pick Jimmy up, she looked at him with complete terror in her eyes. A woman who could guide a missile to a specific place was terrified of a nine-pound baby. Looking down at him, Thatcher realized while he wasn't terrified, he was a little scared. Thatcher's hands could cover his entire head, and he was afraid of crushing him.

"Oh, for heaven's sake. I can see why she's a little nervous, but you, Dr. Thatcher? You've had peoples' brains and hearts in your hands, not to mention those two little Conrad children, and this baby is intimidating you?" Nurse Sally picked up the baby while still fussing at him. "What are you going to do when he's ill? Send him to another doctor? If I hear you doing that, I'll come take him away from you."

"He won't. I promise." Rogen took Jimmy from Sally and held him in her arms. "Oh, he's not as heavy as I thought he'd be. I don't know what I expected, but nine pounds sounds like a lot for a baby."

"It is. They usually come out being around seven to seven and a half pounds. But we get them in larger and smaller." Rogen was given a tiny bottle and a rocker to sit in. "Go on, Mom. Feed him his very first food."

Rogen cried the entire time he took his bottle. It didn't take him long to suck it down, and when she tried to burp him, he laid his little head in the crook of her neck and breathed deeply. He could tell she was like him in some ways—a cat. When she was ready to hand him over, Thatcher sat in the rocking chair and held him on his lap.

"Look how tiny his fingers are. And hands." He pulled away the blanket he was wrapped up in and showed Rogen his feet. "All his toes and all his fingers."

"I love his little fat knees. They'll not be this scar free when he gets a little bigger, I'm betting." Rogen touched her fingers to his cheek, and he tried to take them to his mouth. "He acts like he's still hungry."

"You gonna be an on a schedule or when he's hungry sort of parent? Either way is fine. Just when he's hungry and you feed him, I'd still make a note on the time. Too much will make his belly hurt, and too little will not make him a happy camper." Thatcher looked at Rogen, and they decided to let him be his own gauge of when he was hungry. "Good for you. Whatever you did was going to be the right way, because he's your son. All right. When you guys are ready to get out of here, I can show you how to get him in the car seat and anything else you have questions on. But I'm thinking that when your momma finds out you have a baby in the house, Doctor Thatcher, she's not going to give you a minute's peace until she can babysit for you."

Thatcher was amazed that anyone had children if they had to learn how to buckle a baby into a seat, then into the car. He was a fucking doctor with a doctorate in medicine, and he couldn't get the sucker to work no matter what he did. Finally, he let Rogen do it.

"I've seen these things before, and I looked them up on the Internet for the best one." In less than two minutes she not only had him buckled into everything, but the tarp like thing was covering him and the seat. "It's not a tarp, Thatcher. Stop calling it that."

"Well, that's what it looks like. I have one like it on the back of my truck. It snaps on and everything too. I think I could have handled that part, anyway." She kissed him and told him that she knew he could. "I have no idea why, but I think you're humoring me."

They drove home going the back roads. Neither of them minded, but it took them a great deal longer than it should have. As soon as they pulled into the drive and were carrying all the baby stuff into the house, Thatcher leaned against the post.

"Holy fuck, I'm a father."

Instead of going inside, they got back into the car went to his parents. Neither of them could wait. And why should they have to? As soon as they pulled up in front of the house, Thatcher went inside. He wanted to check the mood of his parents, sure that this would brighten up their moods anyway.

"What's up, son? Did Rogen kick you out already? I knew that I loved that girl. Oh well, Thatcher. You can't stay here—" Dad looked at him then at Rogen, who was carrying everything. When Thatcher took the baby seat away from her, his dad stepped back a few steps. "Thatcher, is that a baby you got yourself there?"

Mom came in too then, drying her hands on a dishtowel. When she saw what he had, she stood back with Dad. It was almost comical, like they were afraid of him.

"Yes, Dad, it is. A son. We just adopted him. His name is James Thatcher Robinson. Jimmy? I'd like for you to meet your grandparents."

Dad leapt forward. Mom came at the seat, crying. And once Jimmy was free of the seat, Mom, Dad, and the baby disappeared further into the house. Thatcher looked at Rogen when she laughed.

"I guess whatever mood they were in, it's better now." They followed the sound of cooing. "I do hope they don't talk baby talk to him, Thatcher. I hate that crap."

He didn't point out that she'd been cooing at him since they picked Jimmy up, but Thatcher wanted to enjoy his child a little more. Rogen would hurt him, there was no doubt about that. Putting his arm around her, they watched his parents with Jimmy. Now they only had to tell her mom.

Chapter 13

Anna didn't like the people in her lab class. She didn't care for a lot of things, she thought with a small laugh. But they all knew that she was smart and hated to have her in the same class as them. With her grades, there wasn't any need for a curve for the others to do better.

Not that she understood that. Why was someone being rewarded for not giving something their all? She worked hard. Anna had learned to do that from the start of her life. Nothing was for free, and people sucked the life out of you if they could. Not to mention money. God, would she ever have anything more than enough to squeak by on? More than likely not.

"All right class. It's about time for us to end fall semester. I know that some of you have signed up for some of the classes offered during the winter months, and a couple of you have asked to be my assistant in the coming terms. The list is on my door." Professor Long was a shit hole, and she didn't care at all for his teaching methods. Nor did she care that he tried to corner every female in his office. Anna figured that she was just too old for him, thankfully. At thirty and in college, she thought she was a rare breed. "Miss Hayes, I'd like to see you for a moment. Could you please come to my office?"

"No." She wasn't afraid to tell him no. He was her teacher, not her father. "I have another class, and I don't want to be late."

The rest of the classroom filed out quickly then. Long sat on the corner of his desk when it was just the two of them. And when she started for the door, he did as well and locked it. Then he pulled down the shade.

"You have been avoiding me all term. That's not very nice of you." She shook her head and told him that she was leaving. "Not until I tell you so, you're not. We have things to…discuss, you and I. Don't you like me? I could say that I'll help you with your grades, but you don't need that, do you? And also, if you correct me once more in this room, I'm going to make life very difficult for you."

"If you don't want to be corrected, then get your shit right." She looked at the door then back at him as he slinked his way toward her. "Mr. Long, you should be aware that I have taken care that I'm not helpless. Not only have I taken self-defense classes, but I'm carrying a gun with me at all times."

"There aren't any weapons allowed on campus, Miss Hayes, I'm sure you've been made aware of that." She didn't answer him, her mind frantically reaching out to any one she could find close enough to help her not have to kill this man by tearing his throat out. "You and I, we can have so much fun together."

"No. I want you to back off and let me out of here." She put her book on the first table she came to; her purse, nothing more than a pack around her shoulder, was put there as well.

"I will kill you if you hurt me. I'm not shitting you. I've put up with enough bullies in my life that I'm not going to put up with a piece of shit like you."

He hit her, right in the face, with his fist. Anna went down just as someone answered her call.

Hello? Who is this? Why are you contacting me?

My name is Anna Hayes. I'm a tiger that is in this area under condition of going to college. I'm in room twenty-seven in the Waldo Building. Professor Long is going to rape me. He's already hit me enough to knock me on my ass. The man told her who he was and that he was close. *Please hurry. I'm—*

This time his fist hit her in the belly. She not only couldn't talk, but she couldn't breathe either. Now he was on top of her, his greedy hands tearing at her clothing and her skin. Anna wasn't going to be able to hold onto her tiger for much longer when she felt something coming, someone stronger than her. The she blacked out.

When she tried to open her eyes, all she saw was darkness. That made her panic, and a voice, soft and cultured, asked her to please lie still. Then he started talking to her, telling her where she was and what had happened to her body.

"Professor Long? He was trying to rape— Did he rape me?" The man said no, he'd tried but he never got that far. "I hurt. Everywhere. I'm a cat—you are too."

"Yes. I'm Doctor Robinson. Everyone here calls me Doc Dawson." She asked him to please tell her what Long had done to her again. "All right. But I'm going to tell you also that this is the third time I've told you. I want you to try and remember now. It'll make me feel better about the head wounds that you have. You have a concussion and several hundred stitches in your head. I don't know what he hit you with, Miss Hayes, but he must have hit you several times.

Your jaw is cracked, but nothing a shift won't heal. However, I'd rather you didn't for a while. The police will need to see you as you are."

"Is he dead? Or the man that came to help me. His name was Robinson too. Was it you?" He said it was his father. "Did he get hurt?"

"Just a little, when he fell trying to get to my brother. Morgan, he's a professor at the college too, is the one that did the actual saving. But my dad, he's loving it. A damsel in distress called for him to slay the dragon." Doc Dawson laughed a little. "I'm going to take the bandages off your face when the police show up again. Anna, they're going to take pictures of your wounds for the trial. All right?"

"He's not dead then." The doctor said that he was. "Then I don't understand. Why would they try a dead man?"

"Because of the people involved in his death. And I can't tell you any more than that right now. But the police are here now. I want you to remain calm with them and tell them what you remember. Not what I've told you, all right?" She told him that she would. "Also, my sister-in-law, Rogen, she'll have a couple of questions for you as well. Nothing major, but she's very much into details. Oh, by the way, is there anyone that I can call for you? Even after you shift, you're going to be sore for a week or so. As I said, he hit you in the head several times."

"No. Please don't call anyone for me." Anna wasn't sure how to explain to him that she wasn't welcome at home any more, and even if she was, it was doubtful that she'd go there. "I'll be fine. I have a nice apartment, and I'll be fine."

"We'll see. All right. I'm going to allow them to come in. If they get too rough for you, just ask for Rogen—she's here for you too. All right?" She nodded again. "Good. Now, I have to go and see to other patients. None of them are as calm nor as pretty as you are."

When he spoke the next time, it wasn't to her but to the police, and a woman who she assumed was Rogen. As soon as the door clicked shut, they bombarded her with questions.

"Hang on a fucking minute. You've had a couple of hours with this. I just woke up." There was laughter from the woman, and it made her feel stronger for some reason. "One at a time. And if you irritate me again, you'll have to ask your questions of me with one of you in here at a time. I have a splitting fucking headache, and a man just tried to rape me today."

"Yesterday." She turned her head to the woman. Anna couldn't see. Her eyes were swollen shut and they hurt when she tried to pry them open. "You were hurt yesterday. You've been in the hospital for an entire day now. I was going to tell you that I had your back in here, but I think you can handle these guys pretty well. Go on, keep them in line and do what you need."

"Ms. Hayes, my name is Andrew Keen. I'm with the local police. I'd like to ask you if you and Mr. Long had a relationship before yesterday." She told him no. "You've never been to his house, never been on a date with him? Nothing?"

"No. Why would you ask me that?" There was silence. "If you don't answer me, my mind is going to make up all kinds of things, and I come from a very scary background. Tell me why you'd think those things. I'd heard about him, the way that he'd have someone come to his offices to talk. But it's never been me. I thought—I guess I thought I was just too old for him."

"No, I don't think that either. He had some pictures of you. In his office and his home." She said she never posed for pictures. "These aren't that sort of picture. There are some with you coming out of a coffee shop. You eating a Danish on a park bench. There are quite a few of them."

"How many?" This time it was Rogen that answered her question. "Several hundred? Are you fucking with me right now? Several hundred? Why would he—? Holy shit. He's the one. It was him."

Pictures were taken then. They were of parts of her body that she couldn't see. But she could feel the tearing of stitches, the pull of muscles that were hurt. And when someone asked her if they could see the bottom of her feet, she asked him why.

No one said anything to her for several seconds, then she heard the door open and close. She wasn't sure that she wanted to be alone right now, but she thought she might have sickened them. Then Rogen spoke, not to her but to the police officer, Keen.

"I told you that she would understand." Rogen laughed. "All right, Andrew, ask her what you want to, and I'm going to ask her the rest. That way we can wrap this up and be out of her life."

"Ms. Hayes." She asked him to call her Anna. "All right, Anna. I'm going to tell you things that are straight up true. Then when you've had enough of me, Rogen is going to fill you in on the rest. However, when you leave here, you cannot under any circumstances tell a soul what she is going to brief you on." Andrew asked if that would be all right. She said yes. "And the bottoms of your feet would be covered in bite wounds. First as a human, which we couldn't understand until today wouldn't match his. He wore false teeth over his own. And of course, we couldn't see those of his wolf."

"Wait a minute. Did you say brief me? Brief me on what?

I don't understand. What happens if I tell someone?" Rogen answered that she'd be as dead as Long was. "I see. And I believe you too. I don't have any idea what is going on. Nor did I encourage or tease him into doing what he did to me."

"We believe you. You're not the first one, as you know. There have been seventy-five complaints about Long. All of them from young women, all whom dropped out of school as soon as Long was proven to have not been the man who had raped them. He is a shifter, wolf, and before he could be examined, he'd shift and—"

"He'd be clean of all the wounds he might have had. The women. Did he take pictures of them as well?" Rogen told her not that they could find. "I don't know if you need it or not, but I have a list of women that I know he's been with. I mean, I'm a cat, as you know, and when he'd come around me, I could smell them on him." She said that it was in her notebook in her back pack.

"It's in evidence, but I'll make sure that I get it. Anything else you can remember or have done?" Anna told Rogen that she carried a gun on campus, she'd been that afraid of him. "Good for you. I think I'm going to like you, Anna Hayes."

After a few more questions, Andrew left them. Anna's head really was pounding, and she laid her head back on the pillow behind her. Rogen asked her if she wanted anything for pain.

"No thanks. I don't react well to them, and I don't take much because I don't want to be in a position that might get me killed." Rogen said nothing. "What have you found out about me, Rogen? I have no idea why, but I think that you're one of those people that does research on other people. We can cut the bullshit, and you can just ask me whatever it is you want to."

"As I said, I like you, Anna." She didn't even bother saying anything. After this, it would be important that she moved on. "I did research you. In depth and completely. Also, you're right, I am one of those people that finds the messiest dirt on people and lays it out for others to use. On you, however, I found not so much dirt as the shit being heaped up on you."

"You got that right. I've had a rough childhood and a rougher life. I'm not a full-blooded Bengal, as you more than likely know. I just turned up as one when my parents had me. They told my parents that it might have been several generations back that a cat was in their family, or just recently. That's all my dad heard, and he kicked my mom to the curb, and me along with her." Anna laughed, feeling the bitterness of bile come up to the back of her throat. "But he forgot that Mother was the breadwinner, and the person who had parents that were wealthy. Good old Dad decided that she could stay with him, be his fuck buddy, but nothing more. He actually called her that instead of Ruth, her actual name."

"You have three brothers as well." Anna started to nod but stopped herself and verbally told her that was right. "Noah Jr. In prison for robbery with a weapon, murder in the first degree, as well as possession of a hand gun when out on parole. David, and he's my favorite idiot of all time, murdered a young woman while she was out with her friends. Then when he realized that he didn't have gloves, he took her credit card and bought them for himself, and a candy bar. He signed the card with his own name. Then there is Buddy. Goes by Bud. At sixteen he was the driver of the car that was used in a drive by shooting. Six people were killed and two more injured. This moron of the highest degree then takes his car to the car wash down the street from his house and tells one of the people there that he just made an easy six hundred bucks for driving the car."

Yes. And that man told his brother, who was the chief of police at the same time. You're right, morons, all of them. And my dad — what did you find out about him that you think I might not know?" No answer. "I don't know why you need to go over this with me. I can't imagine that it would be useful to anyone other than me. Why do you even care?"

"Because, Anna Hayes, you're the mate to my brother-in-law, Morgan. And he's the one that saved your life by killing Long."

~*~

Morgan had never killed anyone before. But he didn't feel bad for doing it the other day either. As he sat in his home, wondering what he should be doing now, he thought about the events that had given him an insight on people that he'd never seen before. Especially Paul Long, a man that he never liked but worked with for a long time. Ten years, he thought.

He thought about the first time he'd heard of what the monster was doing right down the hall from him. When his dad asked him where the room was that Anna was being hurt in, he was two doors down from there in a meeting of his own. Going to the room at breakneck speed, all he saw was a grown man beating a woman with a large statue that he had. At that time, Morgan had no idea who the man was — his back was to him, but he was covered in blood. When he saw her gun lying not a foot from her shoeless body. Morgan just knew that she was dead. That Paul, he'd realized, had murdered her.

"Long, what the hell are you doing? Get off her right now." Paul turned and looked at him. And for as long as he lived, he'd never forget the satanic look on his face. The way the blood from her dripped from his cheek and was all over his face and hands. "I'm going to kill you if you don't get off her. You're going to kill her, man."

"She's mine. I saw her first." Paul's voice was even all wrong, he'd just realized. It sounded gravelly and full of hatred. "Go away, Morgan, and when I'm done with her, you can have a piece too. But wear a condom. They get testy with you if the police find semen inside of her. I'm going to have me a grand old time with this piece of ass."

When he lifted the statue, one that Morgan only just recognized, he was bringing the bust of Beethoven down on the woman's head again when Morgan fired the gun. That too was something that he'd never forget. The sound wasn't that loud at all, but it did make his ears ring. He'd just shot a man in the back. Then Morgan shot him again when Paul got up and came staggering toward him. This time Morgan shot him in the head and he finally dropped. So did Morgan.

His dad had shown up seconds later. It could have been days for all Morgan knew for sure; his mind was still centered on Paul wanting to share a dead woman with him. Dad finally slapped him hard on the face.

"You all right?" He nodded, then shook his head. "Yes, I can see that. Just don't shoot me, son. I'm going to check on them to see if either of them is alive. Don't move. The police is on their way."

The police had asked him a million questions, and Morgan tried his best to answer them all. But his vison kept drifting to the dead man. The woman was being worked on by the medical team that had arrived first, and he wasn't in any position to see her. He wasn't even sure that he wanted to, for as much blood as had been on Paul. Andrew, his friend and a police officer, had spoken to him like he was asking him to go fishing with him. Or have an ice cream. Everything about that day had been surreal now that he could think back on it.

"Morgan, I'm going to have to put you under arrest for this. I know you were saving the girl and all, but we have to go by the books on this one, okay?" Morgan had stood up and staggered a little. "Steady there. I have you. Just let me cuff you, and I'll take you on to the hospital to get you checked out."

"I'm all right. I promise. Andrew, he told me that he'd let me have sex with her when he was finished with her. What sort of sick bastard does that?" Andrew told him to hush up and wait for his attorney. Morgan told him how sorry he was again and again that day.

"I know, Morgan. You're a good man." He was escorted to the cruiser that was just outside the building and sat in the back seat. His dad came to the car and Andrew let him speak to him. "But nothing about the case. I don't want this to come back and bite any of us in the ass."

"All right, Andy, I understand that. Son, I talked to your mom and she's a tad upset. Not with you, but about that poor girl. Don't you fret none. We got your back. Rogen is getting someone to come to the station to talk to you soon." He nodded, suddenly feeling sick. "Just hold on, Morgan. You're going to be just fine."

He was fine after being checked out at the hospital, and then taken to jail, he remembered. They weren't charging him with anything, but Andrew wanted him close so that he could ask him questions if he had any. Morgan laid down on the too small cot and closed his eyes. When he got home, he decided, he was going to shift and then go for a run that lasted the rest of his life.

"Morgan?" Morgan, his mind in a fog even then, had looked up at the man standing there. It had been Dean

Sheppard. "I just found out what happened. Do you need anything? I want you to know that this isn't going to hurt your dean-ship. You killed a horrific person, and I for one commend you for it."

"Thank you. I don't think I need anything. I just want to go home and take a shower." Sheppard said that he could well understand that. "Yes, and thank you for coming down here. To be honest with you, sir. I didn't even think of how this might affect my job. I was just more concerned with the young woman."

"As you should have been. To think, he'd been doing this all along."

That struck Morgan as odd. Even now, two days later, he was still concerned about Dean Sheppard's comments, when he was sure that everyone, including him, had known about Long's horrific behaviors. There had certainly been enough reports filed against him. Not that he'd been trying to kill women, but just that he'd tried to get into the pants of a lot of them. But Sheppard spoke before he could question him about it.

"You go on home, and we'll take care of the press at the school. The school might have a few questions for you, like why did you have a gun in class, but we'll talk about that later."

A few hours later, not only was Morgan showered and cleaned up, but his mom was pampering him a little. But the need to see the woman, he didn't know why, was driving him crazy since he'd been home. He didn't mention it to his parents, but when he could, he told Mom that he needed to take a drive. Blow the smell of death off him.

After driving around for a little while, he'd gone to the hospital to see the woman. Morgan hadn't realized that she was close to his age, only a year between them. But he snuck in the room with her while Dawson was checking her IV's. It was then that he realized not only was she pretty, but she was his mate as well. Morgan went home after that and hadn't left since. Now here he was in his house, still not sure what to do.

Getting in his car, he drove to get himself milk and eggs, neither of which he knew if he needed or not. Then as he was standing in line, ready to pay for it, he felt her fear, or something akin to it. Leaving his little blue basket on the floor, he made his way to her. Morgan didn't know what to say to her if there was nothing wrong, but he needed to make sure she was okay.

"Hello." Morgan had no idea how long he'd been standing there, just staring at her. But when she spoke, he moved into the room. "That wasn't an invite, moron. I just thought you were lost. What do—? Holy crispy noodles, you're him. My mate."

It wasn't a question, but he answered her anyway. "Yes. I'm Morgan Robinson. You're Anna Hayes. I'm so sorry that you were hurt. I did the best I could in getting to you as quickly as I could." She asked him if he'd saved her. "Yes. My dad, you reached him first and he had no idea where you were. I figured out I was right down the hall. May I sit down?"

"No, you're not staying." Morgan smiled and sat anyway. "That sister-in-law of yours, Rogen, have you talked to her yet? She's got some intel on me that might make you want to run in the other direction."

"I doubt it. I'm a dean of studies at the college." She twirled her finger in the air like it was no big deal to her. "And no, I've not spoken to Rogen. And if she had something on you, I really don't care. Whatever it is, we can work it out."

"Look, mister. I don't want you in my life where I have

to be your slave to everything you want. I'm here to go to college and try to make something of myself." He nodded. "Are you addled?"

"Not that I'm aware of. I am rattled, however. Ever since I saw you there on the floor, all I can think about was I'm glad that I could save you." She snorted at him. "Such a pessimist. I was glad that I was able to save you for yourself. And me. But that was later, of course."

"You're a dumbass." Morgan was delighted with her. She was sour and bossy. Anna was not afraid to say what the thought, and she was Morgan's. Forever. "Look. I'm not even a full-blooded tiger. I can tell that you more than likely have had tigers in your family for generations upon generations. I'm not—"

"What are you studying in school?" He knew that he'd thrown her off. Good, he thought, her scent was driving him crazy as well. "I was teaching finance, but I've been promoted recently and given a nice corner office."

She shivered and he told her he was sorry. "It's fine. Good for you on the promotion. I don't have a pedigree. I don't have much of an education. Not now, anyway. My father is in prison, as are two of my brothers. The third one is on his way back there if what I've read about him is true. Not that I give two cents about where he is so long as he leaves me alone. My mother is dead. Dear Dad killed her one night when I was running around in the yard as a cat to entertain the little handicapped boy next door."

"They're not cats, either of them." She shook her head. "Just so you know, the woman doesn't carry the gene for cats. The father does. So if he thought you mom had stepped out on him, she didn't. I'm sorry about your loss."

She only shrugged at him. "I was never what you might

think of as part of their family anyway. So, what do you want now? To be given my permission to run? Go. I don't care." Morgan stood up and she turned her face away from him. "Everyone does sooner or later, I guess."

Pulling her face around to him, he looked her in the eyes. They were a deep green, almost black with the color. Leaning to her slowly, he nibbled first at her lower lip, careful of her wounds, then the upper. She was moaning when he deepened it. Before it got too much more out of hand, Morgan pulled away and sat down.

"I'm not going anywhere, Anna. I have your scent now, and I'm going to protect you with my life from now on." She didn't say anything, but he could tell she was upset.

Morgan hadn't told anyone that she was his mate but Rogen. And she had promised not to tell even Thatcher. So, while he sat there, her face soft from the meds she'd been brought, Morgan told her everything about his family and some things that he probably shouldn't have about himself. But he was happy, and to him, that was all he needed. For now.

The letter

My darling daughter, Rogen. I feel I can call you that because you aren't here to tell me I can't. I've been thinking about you a great deal lately, ever since your mom and I started this hairbrained idea to come and see you and Jamie.

I won't make it. I know that now. I'm sicker every day, and it's getting harder and harder to hide it from your mom. She's become quite the nurse for me too. And she can drive well enough to do so on her own. So long as someone sets up the GPS for her.

We were terrible parents. The worst kind, I think. I'm not going to ask you for your forgiveness because frankly, I don't feel as if I deserve it. I was, as I said, a terrible person. But I would like to ask that you take care of your mom for me. She will be a friend to you — perhaps not a best one, but someone that you can talk to. And I'd like for you and Jamie to do so. For me.

Again, I know that I have no right to ask anything of you, of either of you, but I would hope, in this, you would do this for me. She will be the only woman I ever loved, and the only one that I ever wanted.

I've been thinking about you as a child. My goodness, you were brilliant. It never occurred to me that you were as smart as you have become until you were gone. As I have heard before, you never appreciate anything until it's gone from you.

I do wish there were words I could say that would make you believe how much I'm sorry for the way that we treated you and Jamie. A way that I could make it up to you for all the years that we spent apart. There are none. And if I could think of them, just for you, I'd tell them to you every day of your life. but as you will soon know, my life is at its end.

I write this to you today knowing that in the morning your mom will find me, dead in my bed. And hopefully she'll find me with you at her side. I know that today is the last day of my life. I'm sorry for that as well.

Not that I don't think I deserve to die, Rogen. I do more than most. But I cannot see your face again, not see any grandchild that you might carry and bring into this world. I won't get to touch your cheeks, kiss you when you leave the house, and will never meet the man that you've fallen in love with. I will miss so much more than I ever thought possible now that it's too late for me to make up for all the cruelty and meanness that I bestowed upon you.

Someday, I'd like for you to think of me fondly. And if it's not in your heart to do so, then you thank me for fathering you so that you can hold your own child. Give a son or daughter as wonderful as you and Jamie turned out to be — no thanks to us — to your husband.

You, of all people in the world, would be the best parent in the universe. Because you will take the things we did to you, said to you, and kept from you as a lesson on how not to raise your own children. You will have a legacy to pass on to them, something profoundly your own that I never had anything to do with.

I'm sorry, Rogen, for everything. There are so many things that I could talk about, but my time here on this earth is growing to a close. I will shed my last tear with my love for you, and my last breath will have your name upon my lips.

With all the love that I should have given you, your father, Dad.

Before You Go...

HELP AN AUTHOR
write a review
THANK YOU!

Share your voice and help guide other readers to these wonderful books. Even if it's only a line or two your reviews help readers discover the author's books so they can continue creating stories that you'll love. Login to your favorite retailer and leave a review. Thank you.

Kathi Barton, winner of the Pinnacle Book Achievement award as well as a best-selling author on Amazon and All Romance books, lives in Nashport, Ohio with her husband Paul. When not creating new worlds and romance, Kathi and her husband enjoy camping and going to auctions. She can also be seen at county fairs with her husband who is an artist and potter.

Her muse, a cross between Jimmy Stewart and Hugh Jackman, brings her stories to life for her readers in a way that has them coming back time and again for more. Her favorite genre is paranormal romance with a great deal of spice. You can visit Kathi online and drop her an email if you'd like. She loves hearing from her fans. aaronskiss@gmail.com.

Follow Kathi on her blog: http://kathisbartonauthor.blogspot.com/

Made in the USA
Monee, IL
02 December 2019